AF451359

MUI : THE LITTLE NANNY

PARUL ASHWIN KHARE

Published by

Office : D-328, Defence Colony, New Delhi-110024
Mobiles: +91-9810539784, +91-9833283155
Emails: ganivpanjrath@yahoo.co.in, tannaazirani@gmail.com

Copyright © 2019 Parul Ashwin Khare

ISBN-13: 9789384901790
ISBN 10: 93-84901-79-2

MRP: Rs.325/-

Printed at Thompson Press, New Delhi

PREFACE

When the mountains echoed, its voice was heard in every heart. Living amongst the nature and the very lap of Dhauladhar Mountains with an exciting history entangled in its tale it was hard not to capture all that in words. Life has been with its ups and downs and throughout that I always dreamt of writing to my heart's content, so it was finally
Mui that got me writing. Building the character was easy but tying the history and relationships together took its own sweet time. With this book I hope that the reader can feel the wind in the mountains, the green grass beneath their feet and Mui with the bonds
That she built.

ACKNOWLEDGMENT

A heartfelt thanks to all the loved ones who pushed me
to pursue my dreams.
all the PoWs who will always be remembered.
to my mother in law Manjiri, Shruti my sister & Col
Pande for helping with all the editing and valuable
feedback.
To my parents Hari and Shobha for their unconditional
love.
To my son Parth who now knows that if you can aim it
you can achieve it.
A special thanks to Ashwin my better half for all the faith
and patience.

PROLOGUE

During the 1940s,Benito Mussolini formed an alliance with Adolf Hitler and together they were fighting the rest of the allied forces on various fronts. Hitler's urge for Power deployed Italian and German soldiers in many parts of the world.

The Italian forces were mainly deployed in Africa and the Middle East against the British regime, hoping for the collapse of the British Empire, but in 1941 the US and the USSR entered WWII against the actions of German and Japanese forces. Italy could not match three super powers at the same time and its influence was limited to only the Mediterranean region.

Many Italian soldiers were captured by the British as prisoners of war (PoWs) during Adolf Hitler's passage to power and many more were sacrificed in the name of duty.

With the movement of Japanese troops to Singapore, the British Empire got worried as they had come within close distance of Britain. This forced them to ship the PoWs to various locations all across the world as they could not accommodate the various PoWs in their territory. Some of them were also sent to India and YOL was one such camp in Northern India.

Thousands of PoWs were accommodated in various camps in India, out of which about twelve thousand were sent to the YOL camp in northern India. Many were even sent to Australia and South Africa on the respective governments' request to ss as labourers.

YOL camp was a small camp nestled in the lap of the Dhauladhar ranges. It not only accommodated the PoWs but also provided them with a serene and pristine environment along with other facilities of the camp. Though under supervision, the PoWs were allowed to venture out in the nearby villages, allowing them a certain degree of freedom.

In 1943 when Italy lost the war a lot of changes in Power meant a new destiny for the PoWs. Many new prisoners of war were accommodated in the existing camps, resulting in degradation of facilities provided to these PoWs as only their number increased but the infrastructure remained the same. By 1945 and 1946, the British Empire had weakened due to prolonged war and rising cries for a sovereign India. As a result, PoWs across British India were moved to Australia and South Africa to work as labourers. Many escaped and many more were lost during this time, never to return to their homeland. Even today, the well-preserved remnants of the PoWs can be seen in the camp.

CHAPTER 1

1941 SPRING

MUI

The hilly trail seemed sharper that day as Mui walked through the trenched path towards her home. Immersed deep in her thoughts, she lost her balance and flung the entire contents of her basket on the ground.

"Oh my," she yelped with pain as she landed flat on the hard ground scraping her knee. She pulled herself up from the ground as her eyes circled the area making sure no one had noticed, her moment of embarrassment warily showing on her reddened face. A light breeze hauled her kameez* up in the air, the olive green colour merging into the lush green surroundings. Pushing her kameez down, the wind making it difficult, she dusted her dress and looked at the trees and flowers around her.

"It's so beautiful," she gasped, swirling in the flowery breeze, brushing through the bed of wild flowers. She flung aside her slippers and tip toed on the fresh soft grass, suddenly realizing the urgency to go back home. Despite the weight of the basket slowing her down she still enjoyed the journey and quietly admired the slopes.

Not far now, she thought to herself as she saw her tiny house among the various coloured houses in the distance. Thunksa village was a very small community where everyone knew one another. The houses were few, small and news travelled fast. The houses were coloured in varied shades of yellow, blue and green with slanting roofs made up of black slates.

Mui's house stood at the far end of the village, tall with a rustic aura that made it look elegantly beautiful, though time had withered away a bit of it. A somewhat bright yellow on the walls now gave it a really rustic shadow.

With plaster chipped off from various places to show the bare stones of the wall, it had a melancholy feel to it.

Mui's tall lean figure disappeared into the mountains as she entered the worn-out house which had the aroma of burnt wood and supper. She blinked her eyes several times adjusting to the dim lighting of the room. She saw her frail mother lying on the threadbare but clean sheets on the bed placed in one corner of the room; Mui's rolled up mattress lay next to it on the floor. The other two cornersof the room were occupied by a makeshift kitchen and the rickety three- legged table that Mui had nicknamed the three legged juggler. On the table was a gently lined collection of small stones of various shapes, each of which resembled some animal, gathered scrupulously by her.

The only window in the house was above the table and was scruffily covered with a torn green cloth that had little white flowers. It hung from a rope which strained from the weight of the cloth.

Aisama grunted, drawing Mui's attention towards her bed. Mui walked past her, dragging the weight of the basket behind her as she looked for a place to keep it. The sight of the timeworn table caught her eye. The table with three legs and one short hind leg, probably broken due to the curse of time, had books kept below it to balance it out. She removed two books with a heavy heart, knowing that school and the stories were far from her reach now. She drew the floral raggedy curtain to a side and peeped outside the window.

The light from the sky fell on the majestic Dhauladhar Mountains, creating an aura of peace and grandeur. The colours of pink, orange, yellow and grey engulfed the mountains and sent her into a haze of beautiful admiration. It felt to her as if she was nestled in the lap of the Mountains with the village seemingly distant and the peaks closer. Spring always brought out the best in the drawn out Ranges.

At the age of seven Mui was a very imaginative girl living in the fantasy world of books, having travelled to far more places through them, than in reality. She dreamed of a better world in which everything seemed so perfect.

Another sigh from Aisama meant it was time to give her the medicine that she got from the nearby village. Aisama could always read Mui's face which now seemed immersed in troubled thoughts.

"Mui, I have heard rumours. Are they true?" she spoke with great difficulty.

"Ma, Uncle was saying that they are moving in a lot of sad looking people. He said that the war has brought more prisoners but they don't look anything like us and they speak a language that he couldn't understand. My teacher was saying they are all Italian, coming all the way over from Bombay harbour. He says they are very far away from home."

Everyone in the village had heard of the coat-pant wearing British officers living in YOL camp just five miles away from them. Rumours were flying of distinguished men in uniform and the array of weapons, with a brigade of people coming in the camp every day. They had even heard of the elegantly beautiful women attired in magical clothes and of the skin which glowed like white snow such that even the tiniest speck of dirt could be seen.

Aisama looked more worried now; the war had broken down the country and the people were suffering greatly due to it.

Mui leaned over her mother and gently brushed aside the hair from her face. Aisama gave her an affectionate look; she wondered how much Mui looked like her father. The eyes were as deep and harmonious as his, dark black and immersed in the shadow of dark long eyelashes, which complemented strikingly against her pale white skin.

A shrill voice caught them off guard as Vati scrammed through the door looking a bit agitated; she signalled Mui to go outside and play with her cousins. Living just a few houses away from Aisama made it an everyday affair for Vati to make her presence felt, as she made it a point to visit her sister as much as possible.

Mui smirked as her aunt's resemblance to her mother always amused her, as their natures were strikingly different.

"What do you intend to do Aisama, you can't just lie in bed all the time!"

Vati was never a woman of kind words. Her practical yet well timed sharp words had often offended a lot of people she knew.

Even with her rough demeanour she genuinely cared for her niece and sister, as she was all they had. Her husband Pratap worked as a daily wager which earned him just enough to feed four mouths, which did not even include her sister and niece. Finances were not great for the family of four and one dilapidated small house - the worry showed desperately on her face.

"Think of Malini; the girl lost her father when she was just two, Aisama. It's time to let her go out into the real world. I have been asked to arrange for some help for an officer's wife; tomorrow I will take Malini there," exclaimed Vati without giving Aisama any time to react.

Vati could never call Malini by her short name as it seemed too peculiar to her, although she had named the little girl herself. She stormed out so that no further discussions could be carried out on the topic. Vati's strong mental strength was a boon for her family as this robustness pressed her to walk the two mile dusty road to the British camp every day so as to sell some of the local handicrafts that she made at home. She would also do some menial jobs while in the area, making her an everyday sight for the British officers' wives. This everyday interaction not just improved her English language skills but also eventually led her to become a customary helping hand.

Outside Mui saw Ved and Bhim engaged in a brotherly tiff. She swiftly grabbed both of them and shook them apart. The jolt of a sudden conclusion to the fight took them by surprise. Mui being the eldest among them was always burdened with the responsibility of restoring peace when the situation demanded.

"Grow up you both, what's the fight about this time?" snorted Mui with irritation. The day was not being easy on her.

"He started it," pointed Bhim towards Ved, who rolled his eyes as if to ignore the false accusations.

"Will you two let it go? You are not little anymore," Mui stressed.

"But I'm just four, Ma says I'm small," retorted Bhim with innocence.

Mui could not stop smiling at such a sincere remark as she looked at Ved compellingly.

"Why does he always get what he wants? I'm six and yet I have to listen to him. Ma also always favours him," Ved alleged disappointingly.

Mui patted Ved's back to get him into confidence, "You are the sweetest brother I know," whispered Mui ever so lightly that only Ved could hear; such loving remarks always brought a smile on Ved's face.

Before long everything was forgotten as all three engaged in a game of hide and seek. Mui barely had a chance to hide when she saw Vati storm outside screaming for her children to accompany her back home. Mui looked at her aunt in confusion before dismissing her raucous exit and walked back inside.

Aisama lay dumbfounded struggling to hold back tears, looking at Mui with dismayed eyes. For the next few minutes Mui just listened to her mother explain the intricacies of her aunt's order, nodding every now and then to make sure she understood.

"You know you don't have to go if you don't want to," Aisama said ruefully, knowing clearly that Mui would not refuse.

Their condition was not a secret as the entire village was a party to their affairs. Everyday brought more troubles as Aisama struggled to work and Mui tried to do everything else in the house, perpetually ignoring her studies. Aisama's prolonged sickness had made the situation from worse to desperate. Making ends meet was difficult even with a little help from Vati. Two suppers had now reduced to one and even neighbours had reached their limits of lending. Aisama was uncomfortably aware that Mui was not oblivious to their circumstances.

Mui shrugged her head, "Ma, you need not worry, I'm almost eight years old now. See how tall I have become. Aunty is right! I need to work till you get better. School will have to wait."

Mui smiled sweetly so that Aisama would not get disheartened as she prepared herself for the responsibility ahead. Her shoulder length, dark brown, straight hair fell upon her mother's face as she leaned in to kiss her cheek. Aisama knew there was no other option but to accept whatever was being offered.

Mui reassured her mother before finally running off to tell her aunt of the decision. Vati was elated and rushed back immediately with her entire family to comfort Aisama, knowing perfectly well of her as well as Mui's worries. The untimely reunion of the entire family gave some solace to Aisama. Vati made a vegetable stew with some potatoes and a cabbage that she had picked from her small garden. The supper was light and left everyone a little hungry, but no one uttered a word. The undercurrents in the house were so palpable that even Bhim, who was generally very verbose, maintained a disciplined silence. After saying their goodbyes, Pratap took the unsuspecting children back home, leaving Vati to spend the night.

All three, now alone in the deafening silence, just exchanged sympathetic glances with each other knowing nothing else. As Aisama fell on her bed, Vati unrolled the mattress to accommodate both her and Mui. Before the light of the kerosene lamp gave away Vati fixed her eyes on Mui and put her hand on her shoulder.

"Don't worry Malini, I will be here every day to look after her."

Vati had such assurance in her voice that Mui's worries eluded her for a brief while. Her last night at home was a haze of sleep and anticipation. Mui could not sleep properly all night as the anxiety of separation was too difficult to bear.

CHAPTER 2

ELISA MEEMSAAB

The early morning light caught Mui's eyes as she turned in her bed to face her aunt lying next to her. She opened her right eye while rubbing the other with her fingers; the sight of Vati just next to her was a timid reminder of the parting that she would have to soon endure. Struggling not to fall back asleep, she rose from her bed lightly, trying not to disturb anyone and reached for the door. The sudden creak of the door made an alarming sound which made Mui jump in her shoes. She looked behind and was relieved that everyone was still asleep.

The view of the mountains from their house always soothed her soul. The fresh morning breeze blew through her soft brown hair as she yawned while stretching her long arms. She flipped her hair back in place and heaved a long and heavy sigh fixing her eyes on the scenery before her as if to absorb all that she could. Never had she felt so far away from home as she felt now. A nagging feeling of anxiety took her by surprise as she clenched her hand on her tiny belly.

A sudden movement towards her left brought her back to reality and from the corner of her eye she could see Pratap taking his sheep to graze on the mountains. Pratap's income was very unpredictable, for as and when the work was available, he would earn, otherwise days would just pass by without any real money. The days were hard and the money less, for that's the life of a daily wage worker.

Mui loved the mountains and liked to give her uncle company so she hurriedly followed him, her thin yet sturdy silhouette caught swaying in the brisk breeze.

Pratap noticed her approaching and whistled his sheep to halt, which was sincerely obeyed with a loud 'baa'.

"Mui aren't you supposed to leave for the camp?" asked Pratap puzzled.

"I still have time uncle; can I please come with you?" Mui's innocent yet pleading expression was enough for Pratap to relent and let her come along. Both walked through the grasslands atop the mountain. Spring brought out the best in them as the flowers blossomed and the wind sang. Mui pranced around the sheep singing a local song which made Pratap laugh.

"Be careful Mui there are leopards and panthers here," Pratap warned.

"You have taught me well uncle, grooowwl," Mui made rasping yowls which caused the sheep to run here and there, scared to death.

"You mustn't do that Mui," Pratap shrugged disapprovingly.

"Look how they are running uncle," she exclaimed ignoring his warnings. Pratap followed his sheep and caught them before they could disappear into the mountains.

"Your actions have consequences Mui. One day all this preaching will come to your rescue." Pratap spoke with dignified diligence.

Mui bent down to pet the sheep, a bit embarrassed at her childishness. She knew better and her uncle had taught her well. Immersed in her own world she prodded along, putting out memories of the previous night, enjoying Mother Nature's care. Although the trek was demanding and tough, Mui was the child of the peaks and running through them came as naturally and effortlessly to her.

"Doesn't this look like a heart uncle?" she chirped, picking up a pebble with round edges curved in the middle.

"Yes, it does," Pratap replied admiring her vivid imagination as she pocketed the stone for her precious collection.

As they both saw the sun rise high up in the sky covering the grey peaks in orange and yellow, Mui started to panic, suddenly realising she was late. Almost tumbling down the mountain, she waved her uncle goodbye and rushed back home.Standing outside her house she just stared at the dilapidated shambles of a home as her stomach growled with hunger.

"Oh, I better go inside," she walked back inside reluctantly, giving a desperate glance at the tall pine trees; she would miss this place, she thought to herself.

Mui had been working all her life since her father passed away when she was just four years old. She had seen her mother struggle with even the tiniest of things and suffer in silence as their home deteriorated over time. The idea of working at someone else's house did not trouble her so much as did the thought of parting with her mother, which was creating tremendous amount of butterflies in her stomach.

Vati had just woken up and was rolling the mattress back in its original position. She signalled Mui to start a fire.

"We need to leave as soon as possible. Please be on your best behaviour Malini," snarled Vati to warn Mui that deeds are always judged and misdeeds never forgiven.

She was the only person in the world to call her Malini in such a dominating tone and frankly it scared her.

Aisama, although awake, kept lying on the bed facing the wall so that she didn't have to face anyone. She clasped her eyes shut and covered her head with the blanket but her ears were alert, listening to all the conversations in the house. Vati knew this was her way of dealing with situations, so she did not bother her.

Vati made three thin rotis with the dough that she had kneaded with half-heart early in the morning, making sure there was some left-over dough for her sister. Mui was busy packing. She had bound her precious collection of 3 sets of salwar kameez into a tight bundle wrapped in a thin cloth and was looking around for her doll made from rags. Mui reached for the doll which sat silently on the table and as she picked it up, the sleeves of its dress caught the edge of the table ripping not just the dress but the entire arm of the doll.

"Oh no, not today," she screeched, holding the dismembered doll in her hand as tears rolled down her eyes. Vati alarmed at such disposition, tried to soothe her. "She is just a doll Mui and you are beyond the age for playing with toys," she exclaimed.

The words rang in Mui's ears as she wiped her face and put the doll back on the table.

Even though her stomach growled, she had lost her appetite.

"I won't be carrying you there child, you need to eat," Vati was persuasive, making sure they both ate one roti each.

"Ma, please eat the roti," Mui shook the blanket to get her attention.

"We are leaving Aisama," Vati exclaimed in a loud voice but to no avail, as Aisama merely shrugged.

Mui gave one final look at the covered figure and left without uttering another word,the gush of wind closing the door behind her.

Vati and Mui now began their long tapering dusty trek to the camp area. They entered the camp, aware that various eyes were following the dusty figures they had become. They had heard of hundreds of prisoners being accommodated in the camp and the eyes following them were proof enough.

The camp was a haven for the prisoners. Numerous barracks were scattered along the length of the camp fence on one side. The accommodation on the other end of the camp seemed to be for the officers. The entire area of the camp was lush green, full of trees, flowers and plantations with breath-taking Dhauladhar Ranges visible from all its nooks and corners.

To Mui it was a new feeling of being a worker as everyone seemed to have a job and everything was so meticulously organized. Although the officers' barracks seemed nicer and were further away from those for the prisoners, to Mui it seemed a very nice area for living. Tailored camp fencing with security posts at various points congregated to form one small world in itself.

"What are they getting punished for aunty?" Such innocent words caught Vati off guard as she noticed Mui looking at men in khaki uniform, all dressed alike.

"Shush Malini, it is not your place to ask questions," replied Vati with agitation.

After the surprise of the initial wonders had worn off they concentrated on climbing the steep uphill road covered with pine, deodar and broad-leafed trees on both sides, towards the far end of the camp where officers' living barracks were constructed.

The entire location was like a picturesque dream with magnified splendour of the mountains in the backdrop. As they both approached the officers' barracks, they could see Elisa sitting in the garden with her cup of tea with Captain Hill right next to her. Elisa saw them coming as Captain Hill left for inspecting the duties, aware that it was a household matter best handled by the lady of the house.

As Mui got closer, she was overwhelmed by the exotic looking lady in front of her. Her rose white skin and long golden hair looked so attractive to Mui that she just couldn't keep her eyes off her, almost to the point where it seemed she was staring. She had never seen such a woman in her life. All the men in the village wore Kurta pyjama and salwar kameez was the ladies' attire. Mui looked shabby in her dark blue salwar kameez with half combed hair and dirty slippers. Her awkwardness showed in front of the elegantly attired woman draped wonderfully in a pleasant pink and white laced gown. Elisa noticed the curious look on Mui's face and spoke with comforting words. Her voice was so soft that Mui could not hear it at first and gave a puzzled look.

"Do you speak English child? What's your name?" queried Elisa.

"She doesn't understand English meemsaab, but Malini learns fast and is a hardworking girl," exclaimed Vati in a convincing manner as she pushed Mui towards Elisa.

Vati had the pleasant gift of speaking English due to her regular interaction with English people. Benefits of acquiring the language came in handy more frequently than she knew.

"Mahleenei," Elisa spoke with an accent, repeating it a number of times so as to help her remember another difficult Indian name.

This made Mui chuckle, hearing her name uttered in such a uniquely weird way.

Elisa gave Mui a very approvingly gentle gaze which brought a faint smile on Mui's face. "She is too young Vati; can't you arrange for some older woman?"

Vati heaved a sigh, "Memsaab, she is a hardworking girl, you will have no complaints from her, plea..ea..se," she fumbled.

"Alright, Mahleenei is it?" Elisa retorted looking at Mui.

"Mui," she answered pointing a finger at herself making Elisa a bit more comfortable with the name.

"She is a smart girl. Alright Vati, she may begin today but do explain to her that the work is hard and the hours will be long. I have arranged a room where she can keep her belongings and sleep. Also, she can go back home on holidays or whenever we can spare her. Her salary will be given to you at the end of each month," remarked Elisa as Vati nodded in agreement.

"How much wage would you agree upon?"

"Whatever you think is fair memsaab," Mui was surprised at the tameness of her aunt, who otherwise always seemed so dominatingly fierce to her.

"Twenty five rupees should be good as of now, but if she breaks anything, I will deduct money," Elisa spoke with authority.

"Yes memsaab," Vati looked at Elisa with sincerity, shifting her eyes.

"Follow this road and turn towards the big pine tree; at the end you will see a small room. That is for her, leave her belongings there and tell her to come here for instructions. You may go after leaving her." Elisa left after giving instructions in her crystal clear voice.

Vati took Mui's hand and guided her to the room.

"She spoke too much," Mui retorted.

Vati gave Mui an exasperated gaze. "You must not disobey her, she is what we need right now Malini," she said, clenching her shoulders with both her hands.

Vati gave Mui an uncomfortable hug and left her in the care of Elisa, hoping for the best.

Her heart sinking as she walked further and further away from Mui's room, where she could see her niece standing frozen at the door just staring blankly at the road. The walk back home was a heavy and long one; she needed to answer to her sister.

Vati opened the door to find Aisama curled up on the bed, the roti still uneaten lying indiscreetly near her lean figure. She sat next to the torn blanket, running her hand on her ailing sister's back hoping to comfort her.

"She will start work from tomorrow Aisama, but she will be staying there only. She can visit during holidays or whenever they permit. She will be well taken care of."

Assurance of the unseen future was all she could offer right then. Vati was not going to waste more of her time and energy as she had two children back home waiting for her to return. She rose up and lightly touched Aisama's shoulder signalling her departure. Aisama shrugged just to acknowledge her presence.

"Do eat something," Vati left with a feeling that this was all for a better tomorrow, blissfully ignoring a mother's heart.

CHAPTER 3

THE FIRST DAY

Vati's departure was a sudden realisation of being away from home and the reality of her new shifted life. All of a sudden she felt alone as the truth of the recent events dawned on her. She looked around the room which would be her home from now onwards. The walls were shabby, made of aged rustic looking wood, eaten at places by termites.

The worn out floor was too cold for her bare feet and sent shivers up her spine, making it difficult to stand.

The room had a lone uncovered window; the wooden table below it squeaked even at the slightest touch and reminded Mui of the three-legged juggler. A solitary bed with a light blanket occupied the other end of the room. She shrugged trying to drown the sudden feelings of sorrow, and started unpacking her small bundle of clothes, trying to divert her mind. Unpacking barely took anytime as she placed herself at the corner of the bed looking at the bare window. She glanced through the entire room looking for something that she could use to cover the window. Her eyes caught sight of a piece of dreary old cloth hanging from a hook on the wall probably used for dusting. She reached for it, scanning intricately for its size and hung it delicately on the window, ostensibly pleased with her work, as it made the room a wee bit brighter. Despite her efforts the room had a melancholic feel to it, which made her rush outside for fresh air.

A loud scream from one of the stockades stopped her in her tracks and made her shudder in horror. She had heard stories of prisoners who were forbidden to move around, chained, forever bound and tortured in their enclosed cells.

Scared to her bones she covered her ears with her hands and ran towards Elisa's barrack. Elisa had been in her garden, basking in the bright sunlight as she heard approaching footsteps; she turned around to find a terrified little face. Empathy was not one of her strongest traits, as she wilfully ignored the girl and signalled her to come close so that she could describe to her the work at hand.

Elisa rattled off all the instructions, which confused Mui as it all seemed alien to her. Realising that she had erred in sending away Vati early, to her despair she switched to communicating with Mui in the form of gestures and decipherable signals.

"For today this much work should be enough," Elisa moved her hands to convey her messages which were well understood by Mui.

Mui washed the utensils, washed clothes and hung them out to dry, barely getting a minute to breathe. This in a way was a blessing in disguise for it kept her occupied, and, in the bargain, helped her to not brood about her home.

While gathering the dried clothes she saw Emma and Edward returning from school. Though younger by two years Emma was as tall as Mui; even Edward was tall for a four year old boy. Both looked at Mui with curious eyes, scanning her from head to toe, perplexed with the odd creature in their house. To Mui, Edward had warmth about him but it was just the opposite that she felt from Emma, which made her rather uncomfortable.

"How was school?" was ·Elisa's first question to the children, a daily routine which she never broke.

"Mother... Mother, who is she?" Edward's inquisitiveness was beyond his mother's questions.

"Well she is Mui; she will be taking care of you two from today. Now please no more questions - go inside, change and have your supper." Elisa had little patience when it came to Edward's never- ending questions.

"She looks so dirty mother and smells bad too! Can't we have our old governess back?" Emma pleaded giving Mui an appalled gaze.

This unflinching attention made Mui feel self-conscious as she stood in one corner fiddling with her hands.

"To your room now!" Elisa roared out of impatience.

Their mother's word was always final and the children did as they were told without further inquiries.

Mui finished her work, trying hard not to get in sight of any of the family members, but still there was a peep here and there by the children who were full of inquisitiveness about the new girl.

The day went by as if in a fleeting second and the night brought with it new things to unravel. Mui dragged her tired body back to her shabby room holding a dim lit kerosene lamp in her hand, dreading being alone at night. She kept the lantern on the table hoping that it had enough oil to last the night. The entire room looked haunted to her as it all squeaked from time to time making her jump out of her skin.

She looked around the dreary room trying to imagine a better room with a nice bright light to lift all shadows from the dark. She looked at the rickety table and smiled as she drew an imaginary crochet green cloth on it with lace at the corners.

"I will call you, my juggler's brother." She smiled while looking at the table.

The light in the room grew brighter as the lamp replicated into four magnificently carved lamps standing royally on wooden stools at each corner.

"Oh, this is so pretty, if only the window had golden drapes with frills."

Mui moved her eyes to the window on top of the table as drapes placed themselves elegantly over the window. Even the window which was partially open due to broken hinges seemed to repair itself and stood intact in bright red colour. Mui's eyes were sparkling with excitement moving from corner to corner as the room magically transformed into an exciting sight. Her bed was covered with soft bedding with a thick warm blanket which she wrapped herself with, feeling its fleece on her cheeks. The creaking of the floor turned into soft music and the floor did not seem too cold now as a beautiful rug covered the entire floor. Mui blinked her eyes several times to take in as much as possible. As the light of the lamp flickered, it brought her back to the real world.

She lay awake at night drifting momentarily into sleep, staring cautiously at the lantern which burned till midnight. By the time the light went out Mui had drifted away to sleep, tired by the rigorous day.

Her frail figure lay undisturbed on the bed till a loud howl disrupted her sleep making her tremble in fear, waking her up by the sudden disturbance.

"There is no such thing as a ghost."

Mui recited her prayers hoping that the gods would come to her rescue. She realised she needed to use the toilet but was scared by the prospect of going out alone in the middle of the night. Pain had now taken over as urgency hit. All toilets were a hole dug in the mud outside and at a distance from the living quarters which was covered by thin tin roofs and thatched walls, except for those for the officers, which were luxuries in themselves. Mui reluctantly crept out of her bed still holding onto her blanket, crawling towards the edge of the door. Gathering some courage she peeped outside to make sure nothing was nearby. Knowledge of the wild animals and the local folktales about pahadia, the mountain man, haunted her thoughts as she brushed them aside, quivering.

"Maybe I could do it here only," she was tempted but the fear of Elisa Meemsaab's retribution if she found out, prevented her from doing so. She shrugged the thought, moving outside carefully after dropping the blanket at the door.

She could make out the outline of the toilets at a distance as she walked with a quick pace in the light of the moon. The tall trees swayed in the light wind and made disturbing noises. This, along with their dark dancing shadow, made for a petrifying milieu.

Mui prayed and prayed till she reached the toilet and hastened to relieve herself. Heaving a sigh of relief, she flung open the hinged door, too occupied to go back to her room and froze at the sight in front of her. A tall black panther stood a few meters away from her, so close that she could see its thick black pelt reflecting the moon light, its green glowing eyes fixated at the tiny girl. She gasped for air knowing well that shouting would only alarm the animal and pose more risk to her.

"One day my preaching will come to your rescue," Pratap's words rang in her head as she bent down slowly to pick up a large stone, not to cause a sudden alarm.

The panther, positioning itself for a better chance at its target had shifted a few steps, indicating to her that she had to do what needed to be done either now or never.

"Take this, aaaaaaaaaaaaarrrrrrrrrrrrrrgggggggggggg…!!" shouted Mui at the top of her voice, throwing the stone at the panther. The sudden adroit action from her jolted the panther's confidence and he left running.

Mui stood staring at the retreating panther with relief and then fell on her knees to the ground. "Ma… Pratap Uncle… I did it…!" she cried out, sobbing.

CHAPTER 4

1941, SUMMER

LUCA

Italy was at the brink of another war in 1940 and with Hitler's empire expanding at a rapid pace, she had suffered a great blow at the North as well as the South end. Every man, woman and child knew the consequences and after effects of a war-torn country. Young people were called out to participate and render their services to the country.

Luca looked at his far reaching field as his forehead wrinkled with worries. He dreaded the day he will be called in for his service of the battle torn nation.

Although he stayed just twenty miles from Turin(city in Italy) with his two young boys, a wife and a farm that provided for the bare necessities. He was determined to stay as far away as possible from it all, but the war had reached his doorstep and though he did not understand the politics of Hitler or Mussolini, he was still dragged into the arms of war.

It was early afternoon when he received his call of duty. Looking at both his boys he felt helpless, affectionately putting them both to bed at night.

"Take care of them for me," he held his wife close and cried whole night in the arms of the women he loved.

The next day he left home with the vivid images of his family in his mind and heart.

As part of 11 Artillery Regiment, he was sent to Libya to expand the kingdom of the German empire. He fought valiantly not just for his country but for his family too, for the fear of losing them was greater than anything he could have felt. As always, there were many fallen heroes in the battle who were fortunate not to suffer the pain and torture of imprisonment endured by many as prisoners of war. Luca was among the less fortunate to live the life of captivity when his unit lost the fight with one of the British regiments

At the age of just 25 he had seen death and human greed for power from so close that the peaceful world of his lush green farm seemed liked a distant dream.

"Luca, still in your world?"

Luca was still in a daze from all the movement from Libya to Bangalore port, now as a prisoner of war of the British forces instead of a decorated yet battered soldier.

"Japanese have moved to Singapore. This is why we are being shifted here Luca. They can't hold us in Britain anymore. You see, this means they are weakening. We might get a chance to see our homes again."

Noticing that his words were falling on deaf ears, he just looked at his friend who looked more miserable than many he knew.

Sweat broke on Luca's forehead and dripped down his crooked nose as he looked around at the sea of people surrounding him. He seemed more white than usual, as if all the blood had drained from his face.

His brothers- in-arms were all now mere prisoners in this foreign land so far away from home. He recalled his wife Mia, sons Mario and Antonio - trying to recall their curious yet friendly faces. But it had been two years since he last saw them and drawing a picture in his mind was a difficult task now. He fiddled with the small wooden horse that he had carved for his children. When he was leaving for war, Mario had given it to him as a good luck charm.They called it Lucky.

"When I left them, they were just two and four, Angus, now it's been two years. I'm not even sure they would remember me."

Angus grasped the disheartened expression on Luca's countenance and tried to console him, but he himself had suffered great loss because of the war, so he just sat next to the tall thin man in plausible stillness holding onto the flag of his great nation.

The hustle and bustle of the Bombay port soon vanished as the tired prisoners were marked, sorted and sent to their respective camps across British India.

"Group V, camp 26!" Angus repeated the words written on his wrist. Similar words adorned on Luca's hands gave him comfort as both were herded with thousands of people destined for YOL accompanied by a British officer.

Before they knew it, they were again jostled into the crummy train ride all the way to the hills of Bhagsu near Kangra in the northern-most region of British India well known for its beauty and cool climate. The steam engine bellowed its horn to signal the departure, leaving the station slowly, the engine driver shunning the passersby's eyes which were fixated on the unlikely passengers.

Luca shuddered with great anticipation, hunger and movement.

"We will get through this Luca, and together," Angus' positivity always surprised Luca at the lowest of the times as he crouched closer to Angus in the constricted space. The train was small with only three bogies, each chock full of prisoners, around two hundred of them were stuffed like rats.

The journey was long and the train ride did not make it easy. Kangra station was a sight in itself bustling with curious people, trees all around and the humongous mountains behind. Luca was amazed at the swarm of friendly faces staring at them instead of giving them disapproving looks. The cool breeze passed through his short black hair as he gazed at the curious crowd which seemed pleased to receive the exotic foreigners. Everything seemed so different from his country. People dressed, spoke and even reacted differently.

Everywhere he saw diminutive people wearing pyjama kurta and women in an attire called salwar suit, which he had never seen before.

After the protracted train journey, began the long and tedious foot trek of twenty two kilometres to YOL camp.

Luca was awestruck by the natural beauty, but hunger, thirst and fatigue occupied his thoughts.

The slog began at noon with two hundred men on the road together. It was a hassle in itself. It looked like a herd of sheep walking side by side minded by two British officers on horses, one in front and the other at the rear end, shouting and grunting every five minutes.

The road was carved out of the hill, so it was an uphill climb. It turned and twisted like a snake with fir, spruce and deodar trees strewn at one side of the road and the other side engulfed by the whittled mountain.

With hundreds of feet on the ground even the road shuddered and the sound of the feet caught the attention of every passer-by. Needless to say, it was a treacherous passage as one wrong step and you could easily slip down the mountain into the endless gorges of the mountain and reach heaven directly.

Luca could see the mountains coming closer, his eyes merely caught in the sheer grandeur which was engorged as the daylight sun spread a sheet of buttery light on the mountains which glistened in hues of yellow, orange and grey.

Luca and Angus entered the camp together and could not resist the urge to grasp each aspect of the camp which spread over eight hundred acres of lush green land that had prisoner barracks, British officers' accommodation and many other small amenities. New prisoners were warned about the hardcore prisoners who were kept in enclosed barracks and were given the harshest of punishments. There even seemed to be a small hospital for the PoWs run by the prisoners themselves.

Everywhere they could see khaki uniformed men roaming around doing their jobs. All prisoners were equally eager and looked around like manic owls.

Once the initial anticipation had died down, they were gathered in a line, their details were recorded on paper and barrack numbers were allotted to each prisoner.

A robustly round man sat in a corner, with authority, staring at the entire new lot, shifting his eyes from one prisoner to the next, barely whispering a word or two to the person next to him.

"Don't stare at him," an old prisoner nudged Angus, passing the word of advice with a cautionary look. Angus immediately followed and let his head down moving with the crowd, still a bit curious.

Two sets of khaki shorts and shirts were given to each one of them to first change and then move to their respective barracks. After a tedious few days Luca just wanted a few moments of peace. To his relief, he and Angus shared the same barrack; at least he had one friend here.

Each barrack had twenty double decker beds that smelled funnily of damp wood. Luca changed his clothes and went silently to his barrack and lay on the first bed. He saw Angus just behind him climb up on his bed and gave a faint smile.

He closed his eyes for a few moments as the image of Mia, in her long floral printed dress, her black locks swaying in the flowery breeze as she tended to her flowers in the garden, came to his mind; Mario and Antonio running from inside the house into the arms of their mother smiling blissfully. Tears rolled down his eyes as the reality of his existence started to haunt his dreams.

"It will be fine Luca," Angus stared down from his bed, tilting his body in an awkward position. With no reply in sight he climbed down, standing just few inches away from Luca. He laid his hand on Luca's shoulder, relieving him temporarily of the pain.

"I will be fine," Luca smiled meekly and turned so as not to face Angus, dismissing him prematurely. Lucky lay lifeless near his deflated pillow as he drifted back to his life in Turin.

That day everyone in the barrack laid perfectly still, not even a single sound could be heard; realisation was settling in that they were prisoners.

33

CHAPTER 5

LATE SUMMER, 1941

LIFE IN YOL CAMP

Luca along with other prisoners started acclimatising to the new environment. The camp was meticulously managed and handled by the prisoners themselves, distributing and executing duties that befitted them the best. Doctors, nursing assistants and others who had worked in the hospital had already established a makeshift hospital for PoWs. Rest of the prisoners took care of duties like cooking, cleaning, gardening, rationing and many more.

Each day brought a brigade of people, who brought not only more stories of the world beyond YOL but also a part of their homes which seemed to be fading away with time, even in memories. Camp had pleasant weather with the sun shining in the day; but the nights were harsh and grew colder, bringing with them the misery of cold climes.

It was a well-drafted and well-equipped camp even with the meagre means they were given. Food might not have been the greatest, but it was provided. Fruits and rations were in ample supply.

Life in the camp was very dreary - the same routine and monotonous work every day followed by the same the next and the day after. Luca was an adventurous man and the dull life of the camp brought the realities of captivity back. The library was a shrine to him as he buried his entire sorrow in the books and forgot the miseries of imprisoned life.

"YOL - Your Own Lines, these idiots… As if this gives us a sense of belonging… Calling it YOL only deflects us from the point that it's a prison camp!" Angus at his usual best. Luca ignored his remarks and engrossed himself in his work as a gardener.

"Will you look at me?" Angus was annoyed.

Luca looked him and caught Captain Hill at the far end doing his daily check of the prison barracks. Walking behind him was his brigade of British & Indian Soldiers, trailed by trifling Lavera Ricci, appointed redundantly as prisoner commander.

Lavera was a shrewd man and was despised by every Italian prisoner in the camp. His rules seemed more like those of a dictator than of an appointed monitor, afterall he himself was a prisoner, but it was the canny ploy of Captain Hill to appoint a prisoner as warden of other prisoners. Lavera was a strict observer and even a stricter punisher. He kept a keen eye on the movements of all prisoners and would not spare anyone of the adversity he could cause if caught doing things against his wish. Angus disliked him the moment he saw him scrutinizing everyone on the first day they came.

Luca and Angus yearned for the free life and so, on rare occasions when Lavera was in a pleasant mood, they would get the permission to go looking for it in the village outside of the camp, giving them a brieftaste of the life they once had. They would roam around like foreign tourists, interact with the locals and forget the fables of their home, although Lavera made things difficult for them from time to time. In his book there were no favourites, only favourite days, so everyone danced to the tunes he would sing.

"I wish I could make his life as miserable as he makes it for others," Angus tried to conspire.

"Don't do something stupid," Luca warned, ignoring the outrageous remarks as he fluidly moved to do his gardening job. He was a farmer after all, being close to plants made him feel desperately closer to the sheer memory of his farm, wife and children.

Angus was impervious to Luca's preaching and carried out in his mind the plan to disturb Lavera's life in a small way.

Angus walked briskly towards the kitchen to do his routine work with a plan in place. Peeling potatoes like any other day, he waited for the cook to finish the food preparations. The entire cookhouse smelt of chicken with vegetable stew, one plate specially kept aside for Lavera with extra bread and butter. As he enjoyed a special position, he demanded an extraordinary treatment.

Angus looked around to make sure no one was paying attention and poured the entire contents of the paper pouch in Lavera's bowl of stew,mixing it frantically with a crooked smile on his face. He then carried on his duties as if nothing had happened.

Angus spent the afternoon meal in mere anticipation, which was noticed by Luca.

"What have you done Angus? You seem pleased with yourself, which is always when you are up to something." Luca looked deep into Angus's eyes, trying to read the secret of his mischievous smile.

"You will know soon enough," Angus smiled taking a large bite of stew, leaving Luca wondering.

While walking back to work, Luca noticed the groups of men clustering up as if some show was going on. Angus's head bobbled to get a better view when they saw Lavera, red with sweat pouring down his forehead, rushing to the toilet seeming as if he had been there a few times already. They both stood there to witness the circus as a few more men joined the event. Lavera went in and out of the toilet like a lightning bolt. Shallow chuckles were now transformed to loud laughter as Angus held his stomach to control himself.

"I'm going to burst out laughing today," Angus retorted. This made Luca smile with a little worry for Lavera whose face by now had reflected all possible shades of red, growing darker and darker each time he rushed back to the toilet. The last time he just peeked outside the toilet door and went back inside again closing it with dismay; this time he didn't come out for two hours.

"Sto per morireoggi (I'm going to die today). God please just take me today. Stop this torture! I want my mother!" Everyone could hear disgruntled sounds coming from within the toilet.

Lavera finally came out of his hiding looking like a pale shadow of his usual plush round self. He brushed the amused crowd aside and went directly to his room. After that day he was less harsh and quieter but it only lasted a week, after which the after-effects of God's wrath on him subsided to the practical conclusion that someone had played a trick on him. It was a solid victory for Angus who continued his ploy to take Lavera down.

CHAPTER 6

AUTUMN, 1941

It had been months since Mui had come to the camp but it felt like years to her. The entire camp was engulfed in hues of orange, yellow and brown. The air smelled of fresh harvest as the trees shed the leaves with quaint demeanour of the fall. By now Mui had become accustomed to the customs of the house, and living among prisoners didn't cause any uneasiness. The voices from the stockade also became a matter of routine, but still, it sent shivers down her spine. Mui would spend her days doing household chores and looking after the children.

She had grown fond of Edward who was such a fine gentleman with exquisite manners. Emma, just one year younger than Mui,never liked her but still tolerated her as her nanny, making her life a little miserable whenever she got a chance.

"You smell really bad, sit as far away from me as possible," Emma said piqued at the shabbiness of Mui. She was never clean enough for Emma's taste. Mui looked down at her dress, ashamed of being inferior to this princess of a girl; but Edward never saw any flaw in her although he was the youngest of them all.At the age of four he was a delightful young man and had a fondness for Mui that she cherished.

"Mui why are the mountains so big?" he gestured his hands towards the mountains. Mui listened carefully trying to understand the words by his tone.

Edward understood Mui's predicament and spoke slowly with perfect hand actions to explain to her what he meant. Mui's diction in the past few months had improved but still to understand a whole sentence took time. Elisa was precise with her commands so it was easy for Mui to pick up on the meaning. Contrary to that Edward had his endless tales, comprehension of which would seem like a humungous task.

"Sun hide in mountain," Mui explained, letting her expressive eyes do the rest of the talking, her right hand moving towards the sun as Edward's eyes followed all the way over to the mountains. Mui's imperfect English was encouragingly accepted by Edward, who unknowingly yet favourably helped improve her language skills.

"Come Mui, come I want to see the sun from over there. Can we also hide behind the mountain? Emma won't be able to find us there," chuckled Edward with mischief.

"Time go home," Mui's eyes sparkled which had a sobering effect on Edward.

"No please some more time," he pleaded but to no avail. He relented, following her back home leaving the greens behind.

"You are my friend Mui!" Edward gave Mui a warm hug wrapping her legs with his tiny arms. Mui had never got so much affection from anyone other than her mother; she bent down to hug the little man before sending him to the house for his meal.

It was the end of the month and she was expecting Vati's arrival anytime soon but her aunt was running late today and it worried Mui as she would generally reach by noon. She leaned on the entrance door letting her eyes wander, looking for her aunt.

She looked forward to seeing her aunt at the end of every month to take her back home for a day and also to collect her monthly wages set at 25 rupees, most of which was spent taking care of Aisama. That one day of every month always brought a smile on her face as she could be a child again, play, get dirty and run like the wind towards her freedom.

Vati hustled to complete her errands knowing perfectly well that Malini would be waiting for her.

"Malini would be worried by now, I am so late," she recited again and again hoping that it would help her to finish things faster. By the time she made it to the camp it was way past noon.

"One day that child gets and I have fouled half of it," she cursed herself. She made her way to Elisa's house hoping for a very short encounter as these monthly meetings were overshadowed by Elisa's long list of complaints. Elisa was having her afternoon tea in the garden as Vati walked in to greet her, noticing Mui standing excitedly at the door.

"Yes, wait I will get her wage. You are late today."

Elisa's discontented tone always lived up to her expectations. She walked back inside giving Mui the opportunity to run towards her aunt and greet her briefly. Vati waited for a few minutes when she saw Elisa coming towards her with the money. She put it on the table, signalling Vati to pick it. She followed as instructed and took the money, holding it tightly in her hand; it seemed a little less which confused her as to the reason for the sudden reduction in money.

"She breaks more things than she works for. Tell her to be more careful otherwise I will deduct more next month," Elisa turned away, leaving the room in arrogance.

She could never appreciate the little girl's hard work, thought Vati to herself. Mui was partly hiding behind the door listening to the humiliation that her clumsy work had brought. Vati gave Mui an encouraging glance, signalling her to come with her.

"Cheer up, you will do better, don't be disheartened. Let us buy you a toffee and some biscuits. What do you say Malini?"

She just smiled at the very idea of the yummy treats.

"May we buy Ma a few meters of cloth Aunty? Her clothes seem so worn out, she would be so pleased," cheeped Mui with optimistic fervour.

"We can Malini, but who will stitch it? I don't have any time," reasonableness never eluded Vati.

"I will Aunty, Ma had taught me and my skills can do with some brushing up. Please…," pleaded Mui as Vati gave in to a child's sensible demands.

Vati nodded, bringing a sparkle in Mui's eyes. Both walked to the market outside the camp area, Mui picking up a pebble along the way.

"What does this look like now?" Vati remarked with a look of disapproval as she did not understand this leisure pursuit. Mui hid the stone in her pocket listening mockingly as her aunt tried to dissuade her from this futile activity.

 Although it was a small bazaar, it had everything that one could need. Shops lined both sides of the tiny street with little gaps between each shop. Brightly coloured hoarding boards adored the top entrance of each shop primarily depicting the nature of the things sold. They entered a tiny shop which had no doors, just an open entrance with piles of coloured cloth lined in the corner. The shopkeeper, a middle-aged, pale and stout man sat towards the entrance, his half bald, oiled head shone in the light of the day. Wooden racks behind him were all lined up with different varieties of fabric. He watched carefully as the two young, determined women entered his shop.

"What would you like to see today?" he smiled at them with warmth.

Mui had never been shopping before and the excitement of it all made her stammer as Vati pressed her to express her wishes to the nice gentleman.

"Can I have some cloth? I want to make a salwar kameez for my mother," Mui finally muttered the words, which ran through her mind in a loop.

"What kind would you like child?" Mohandas spoke very softly bending down to Mui's level to better hear her desires.

"Do you have ones with flowers on them? My mother loves flowers. It would really cheer her up," Mui spoke with absolute clarity in her mind.

"Yes, child but what kind of fabric would you like or I can show you some pieces and you can select from that." Mohandas perceived the novelty of being a first time buyer from Mui's face.

"Yes, thank you," Vati intervened cutting the conversation short. They spent the next half hour looking through stockpiles of various fabrics, finally picking out a beautiful black printed woollen cloth with small red roses on it.

"You would need 5 meters for a salwar kameez. Should I cut it for you?" Mohandas spoke patiently as he gathered the fabric for measurement.

"Yes, how much would that be?" Vati said, mindful of the price.

"It would be twelve annas per meter." Vati was taken aback by the price as she ran the numbers in her head. Twenty rupees was all she had for the entire month and taking out almost four rupees was difficult to fit in her budget.

She did not want to disappoint Mui but there was no other option; if only she had that extra five rupees.

"I'm sorry but we can't buy this today," she said feeling embarrassed.

"But Aunty….," Mui was cut short by her aunt's gesture to keep quiet. Mohandas could sense the trouble both of them were going through; his face remained expressionless while the two women sorted out the situation.

"Today is a special day so I will give you the whole cloth for two rupees," Mohandas smiled from ear to ear while giving the good news to the polite girl, barely making any money from the sale.

Mui was elated and couldn't believe her luck. Even Vati was astounded with disbelief at the kindness of the stranger.

"Thank you uncle," she choked on her words as her eyes shimmered with hidden tears.

Vati handed over the amount with pride and got the cloth wrapped in sheets of paper, handing it over to the overjoyed Mui, who held it like a prized possession.

"I'm Mohandas, what is your name child?" he smiled curiously.

"Mui" Her innocent smile had captivated his humble soul.

"Mui, I hope to see you soon." He nodded politely and shifted his attention to the next customer.

Both of them, contented with the purchase, went to the next shop, picking up some candies and a small packet of biscuits. Mui counted the number of candies in her pouch, hoping that they would be enough for everyone. By the time they were finished, the sun has started to set with the sky turning from shades of blue to pink.

They hurried back to the village reaching just before night-time. Mui hopped towards her house, tightly holding the gift close to her heart. When the house came in sight, she sprinted to reach the door with Vati running far behind trying to catch up.

Mui flung the door open to find Aisama lying on the bed shifting every now and then with discomfort.

"Ma, I brought you something," she flung the gift on her stunned mother.

"Open it, open it!" Mui couldn't wait for Aisama to open the wrapped packet and tore the paper herself out of excitement. "See, do you like it? I will stitch it for you today itself." Mui looked at Aisama trying to read her expression.

"It's beautiful Mui, thank you." Aisama hugged her with all her heart, holding her lean figure so close that she could feel her heart beat.

Vati walked in to find Mui in her mother's embrace. She kept silent and slid out to get her family for supper. Aisama spent the next few hours listening to Mui talk about life in the camp, organizing her stone collection, which still rested on the three-legged juggler, serenely waiting for its owner's attention and stitching for her a wonderful salwar kameez. She spoke adoringly about Edward who became the centre of her stories, making Aisama glad that at least Mui had one friend there.

CHAPTER 7

UNUSUAL FRIENDSHIP

EARLY WINTER, 1941

The mountains glowed in the sunlight, making the snow sparkle on top, marking the beginning of winter. The snow-clad peaks spoke salubriously of the cold climes of Dhauladhars. But for Mui every new day brought memories of her mother Aisama who seemed paler and thinner the last time she saw her.

The early morning breeze slipped through the nooks and crannies of Mui's room and swept through her thin blanket. She held it firmly but the chill seeped through her blanket making her shiver with cold.

"There is still time," she mumbled to herself crawling up in her bed holding the blanket tighter to let the warmth in.But she couldn't fall back to sleep and finally gave in to the noises coming from outside.

"Good morning, Jugglers brother. Are we still rickety?" She was amused as the table creaked in response, her new stone collection neatly lined up on the table. She walked towards the door still wrapped in her blanket.Watching the prisoners do their work always fascinated her as their life seemed far more interesting than her own. She stood there for a long time engulfed in the morning rosy wind, listening to the wood being chopped, stones being carried and many other tasks being accomplished till it was time for her to go to work.

She crossed the garden to find a new face pruning the roses. Captain Hill's garden was well tended to with various flowers, velvety green grass and a small orange tree in the corner. The hedge was dense and grew like rapid wildfire that needed extra trimming once every two weeks.

She scrutinized the stranger inquisitively, noticing the crooked nose, the khaki uniform and such ominous eyes. He smiled uncomfortably, aware of being examined.The last gardener never spoke a word to Mui, let alone smile at her. The sudden awareness of her action made her blush as she rushed back inside, cautiously watching the new man from afar. For the next few weeks she saw the man several times.He seemed to grow fond of the little girl, always exchanging friendly smiles but never having the courage to speak.

One bright sunny morning while pruning the shrubs, he saw Mui come to set the garden table for tea as she passed her routine smile at him.

His eyes followed Mui's movement and in a matter of a second he tripped and fell in the still wet sludge, covering his entire face and half his clothes in muck, bawling for help.

"Oh, are you alright?" Mui's words were interspersed with chuckles. As she went close to him she could not stop laughing at the sight of this tall man drenched in mud, his crooked nose peeping from behind the mud covered face. It was such a hearty laugh that even he started laughing at folly of the situation.

"Luca," he said pointing towards him. Mui understood and gave him her name.

From that day onwards she looked forward to meeting the man who eluded her of the sorrows that engulfed them both.

***

LATE WINTER, 1942

"Mui get some biscuits from the market and don't take a lot of time," Elisa raised her eyebrow in warning handing over the money to Mui.

"Yes, memsaab," she replied and ran to the market, beaming with happiness to finally meet Mohandas after a long time.

She crossed his shop several times and then finally peeped inside with a mischievous smile.

"Ah, so here you are. I was wondering if I had seen a ghost," Mohandas replied with an amiable smile.

"So what are we doing today?" he continued.

"I just have to get some biscuits from the bakery but I have to rush back since she will not be happy if I come late," she replied with a bit of sorrow.

"Not to worry child, I will accompany you to the bakery."

He was a kind man and even kinder to Mui since he saw his daughter's reflection in her. They both walked towards the bakery in silence as she noticed his dismal face. She remembered the date and felt embarrassed.

"It's her birthday today, isn't it?"she spoke with empathy.

"Yes," he replied.

Mui's entry into his life had helped cure his ailing heart. He had lost his daughter and wife to the misfortunes of fate, shattering his small world. He was so heartbroken that he could never take on another wife or even think of having a family due to the sheer fear of losing them all over again.

"I'm so sorry, uncle." Mui did not know what else to say to comfort the grieving man.

"What kind of biscuits do you want Mui?" he changed the subject and his attention towards the task at hand as she chose the variety she wanted. They both walked back to his shop, Mui holding his hand warmly.

"Goodbye. She wouldn't want you to be unhappy."

Her words tore at his heart and he smiled meekly at the wisdom of this young child. She passed a gentle smile at him before running back to the camp, holding the packet of biscuits tightly wrapped in her arms.

Mui crossed the garden to find Luca trimming the hedge with a frown. She smiled as she put away the biscuits, noticing the sullen expression on his face. Over the last month she had gotten to know this soft man and his life from very close. Although language was a barrier, meanings were conveyed through the language of friendship and frantic hand gestures, which always amused Mui.

"It's Lavera again, I know it. I will pray to God that he should punish him," Mui retorted.

"No… Miss family," he replied with as much diction as he could remember, fiddling with Lucky in his hands.

"You know Luca, this place is really cursed."

She paused to give it a dramatic effect focusing her eyes on him, using hand gestures along with the words to make sure he understood.

"It was called Papi Nagri or Sin city," she continued.

"Huh?" Luca sneered with a hearty inquisitive chuckle, raising his eyebrows.

It was usual for new myths and legends seemed to arise every day from the village people. Angus had warned Luca of folktales and villagers' stories that had no resemblance to reality; but these stories riveted Luca and he encouraged Mui to tell them to him in a most appealing manner.

"It was said that the king of Mujetha fell in love with a damsel and kidnapped her against her wishes. So, she cursed him to live a life of solitude and unhappiness. It is said that whoever comes to live in YOL will carry the same curse."

Mui spoke with a terrified yet worried tone knowing perfectly well that she and Luca both were victims of the sacred curse.

"No worry, I beat out curses," laughed Luca at the conjured tale, almost managing to speak correct grammar.

Mui was awestruck by the questionable super powers of her friend but was also glad that she could ease his sadness. She passed him a smile,which was reciprocated with a friendly nod of his head.

Luca was done with his work and left after he bid adieu to his little friend. He walked towards his barrack holding Lucky in his hand, thinking of the tale he was just told, waiting for Angus to pass a rhetorical comment. In the past month he had seen this little girl being caged with the weight of adulthood. It seemed to him that she had forgotten to be a little girl, the pleasures of childhood eluding her.

That night Luca wondered over the miseries of war, as Angus listened politely.

"I am reminded of my family when I see her. There is a sad yearning in her eyes which draws me to her" Luca's graze fixated on Angus.

"Siamo entrambi prigionieri di guerra Angus, noi con la forza e lei per scelta (We both are prisoners Angus, us by force and she by choice)."

These words echoed in Angus's mind like screams that night.

CHAPTER 8

SPRING, 1942

TALE NOT TO BE TOLD

Emma had just finished reading the Cinderella story and was fascinated by the fantasy world of lovely princesses and charming princes. She narrated the tale to Edward and Mui in a way which seemed almost blunt, lacking the sensitivity and the theatrical effect that truly make for great story telling.

"Mui please tell us a story," begged Edward, to Emma's displeasure.

"Yes, Mui tell us a story. I'm sure village people also have charming kings and queens living among them," sneered Emma.

"Really?" Edward's curiosity jumped with excitement. Mui looked at him with warmth, ignoring Emma's acerbic remark.

Mui closed her eyes thinking deeply of the story she could tell them but her fantasy world was clandestine to her, meant only for her eyes and ears. The only tales that she had heard of were mythical folktales that her aunt and mother had told her, which honestly, thrillingly scared her. After repetitive pleading by Edward she reluctantly began her tale about the Man of the Mountains (Pahadiya) who guarded the sacred temple of Mountain god at night in Thunksa village.

"Every night the villagers would put their offerings in the temple and plead to God that the Pahadiya should protect the town. One such evening, two men went and stole the sweets and money that were put in the temple as offering. That night when Pahadiya saw that the offerings had been stolen, he grew angry and went about in town calling out the names of the thieves," she spoke in a mystifying voice.

"When everyone awoke, Pahadiya had already gone with the men who had stolen the sweets and money. It is said that the two men were never found and even today the cautionary warnings of Pahadiya can be heard at night," she continued with a daunting tone managing to create a melodramatic effect.

When she was finished, she looked at the children who looked scared. Edward's eyes were shining with tears. When Mui tried to console him, his voice grew into loud wails that alarmed Elisa and she barged in to take control of the situation.

"What happened here?" Elisa fumed.

Before Mui could defend herself, Emma narrated the whole story to Elisa who just stood shocked and enraged at the whole idea. She gave Mui an infuriated look and controlled her temper, aware that the children were watching her.

"Mui leave the room and go to your quarters; you are not to interact with the children for two days and no mention of such stories in this house," she screamed as her usually modulated voice thundered with irritation.

"Mother, I told her not to tell such a tale, Edward is so scared."

Emma pointed at Edward, who ran towards his mother latching on her dress and rubbing his tears into the folds of her gown. Elisa swallowed her anger and grabbed Edward by his wrist, taking him out of the room, gleefully followed by Emma.

"That disgraceful little girl," Elisa retorted leaving Mui alone in the room.

Mui was disheartened, trying to understand the reason behind such a fierce reaction. Her eyes now glistened with tears, as she shoved them away with the corner of her sleeve and went to her room to suffer in silence.

Her room was her solace but with time it resembled more of a cold haunted house than a liveable space. She crawled up into her bed trying to let her imagination run wild but the disturbed peace in her mind and the empty stomach hindered that distraction, her eyes were weary from the day's work. She let her eyes rest for just a minute but before long she had fallen in a deep slumber, only to be awakened by the crowing of the roosters in the morning, still feeling hungry as her stomach growled.

"Mui get some biscuits from the market," Elisa instructed as Mui looked at her with pleading eyes. Captain Hill was sitting right next to her for their morning cup of tea in the garden.

"You know the punishment Mui. You will get your meal when you behave properly."

Elisa was a strict woman as Captain Hill nodded in agreement. Hill's military background always held him back from being compassionate with others; his rule was simple, 'bear it till you make it'.

Mui left with the money in her hand almost wanting to steal a paisa or two just to fill her stomach, but her mother had not raised a depraved girl and she would dare not dishearten her. Passing through the market she walked past Mohandas's shop as he sprinted to catch her.

"May I walk with you?" Mohandas had exquisite etiquettes that always bewildered Mui; education is not always needed to be kind. She nodded her head in agreement as they both walked silently towards the bakery.

She picked the biscuits and paid the money, holding on to the change that the shopkeeper had given her. Mohandas had been sentient to her eyes which had such longing and comprehended her state from one look.

"Wait here, I forgot something inside," he said before leaving her outside the shop.

She stood there for a few minutes before Mohandas came back beaming, with a paper wrapped packet, gently passing it in her hands.

"Here take it, these biscuits are for you. I always forget that I don't really like sugar," he smiled at her.

She was elated at the sudden gesture of benevolence and opened the little wrapped packet, taking out two biscuits.
"Here," she graciously handed over one biscuit to him and they both munched in companionable silence.
With some food in her stomach and a friend in her story she ran back to the camp.

CHAPTER 9

SUMMER, 1942

MITI

It was a warm summer day with cottony clouds in the bright blue sky which artistically made a magnificent view. Elisa sat in her garden with a hot cup of tea, admiring the scenery.

Low steps caught her attention and she turned towards the place from where the sound was coming. There stood a stunned street dog with the most curious look in its brown eyes. Its coat was a beautiful shade of light brown but it was so skinny that its bones were visible.

"Argggggggggggg, shoooooo," Elisa said scared, jumping in her place. The dog just stared at her, sniffing cautiously as he moved closer to her chair.

She moved back slowly, her ego too big to succumb to a petty animal.Her eyes fixated on the animal as he started to come closer, smelling everything in his way. The awkward situation almost made her yell for help but she controlled herself, correcting her posture to ward off the damsel in distress signals.

The dog did not seem bothered with the attention as she pranced around the garden looking for some food. By this time Elisa had almost reached the wall and was leaning against it, watching the stray animal ruin her garden.

"Mui, come here,"she whispered through the window, hoping to catch her attention. The sudden sound distracted the dog as he looked at the tall figure. He paced himself, coming closer to the lady.

"Eeeekssss, go away, go away!!!" screamed Elisa with the meekest voice, hopping on the spot. Her composure now

54

gave way to the distressing situation as there was not much she could do.

The heel of her shoe broke and she fell flat on the ground, surprising the dog that was now still, looking inquisitively at her. He sniffed her shoes and then licked the heel which had a piece of cookie stuck on it. Elisa's face now turned from scared to horrified as she picked herself up, dusting away her clothes.

"No, no, go away, go away!" she screamed scaring the dog, who now took a few steps back in caution.

The screams alerted Mui as she came rushing outside, amused by the situation. Elisa was leaning back against the wall and the dog was a few feet away, wagging his tail at the new comer.

Mui shifted her eyes from her meemsaab to the innocent animal, moving lovingly towards the dog.

"It's ok, come here."

Mui caught hold of the dog and tied a rope around its neck as Elisa heaved a sigh of relief.

"Take that thing away from here," Elisa instructed Mui.

The dog was then carefully taken out of the garden and into Mui's room. She petted him lovingly and gave him some bread to eat, which he ravished instantly. He licked the floor for crumbs and then looked at his saviour with the most adorable eyes for some more treats.

"This is all I have right now," she patted him as he licked her toes and snuggled up next to her on the floor, falling asleep.

"You too are away from family, aren't you?" Mui spoke caressing his dull coat. She waited for sometime but as she got up to leave, the dog woke up and started following her out.

"No, no, you stay here." She signalled him to sit but it was of no use as he ignored the gestures, confused as to their meaning. She laughed at the sincere friendship as she held his rope to take him out.

"What can we call you? Hmmmmm…. Miti!" The name reminded her of his brown coat and how it resembled mire.

The next few days Mui spent in the splendid company of her new pet which was introduced to Luca as well. In order to not get caught with Miti, she would sneak around the house and the camp to avoid snooping eyes. Even Miti had grown fond of his new owner, trying to follow her around wherever she would go. It had become difficult for Mui to sneak in food for Miti with his growing appetite. From the timid little dog that she had found a few days ago, he had gained enough health to look strikingly beautiful and his lack lustre coat now shone with health.

It was a special Sunday as the family had planned a picnic in the nearby forest area, a task which was generally accomplished on foot with the help of a brigade of people, a few carrying guns and most of the others carrying essentials that would be needed to make for a good and comfortable picnic. Foldable table, folding chairs, table cloth, lunch basket, sun umbrellas were among the few things being towed for the small picnic. It amused Mui to see the number of people engaged in planning an event which could have been handled by just a few. But that was the Power of Captain Hill and he, like any other man before him, liked to show off.

They all reached the picnic spot before noon and most of the labour force was used to set up the picnic. Most of the men were then instructed to return to the camp while a few remained with guns for safety.

The picnic was set next to a small forest lake which arrested Emma's attention as she stood frozen, captivated by the mesmerising beauty. Emma looked around the magnificent lake, the reflection of the tall pine trees crystal clear in the still water. Her eyes now deflected towards the slow murmurs, annoyed by the sudden disturbance. There stood Edward on one side, chattering away with Mui who also seemed absorbed in the conversation.

"How is Miti? He has become so plump; I want to see him please," pleaded Edward. There were few people who were aware of Miti's existence and Edward was one of them. He loved the little animal and would try to see him whenever possible.

"He is good Edward. Next time I will take you to meet him," Mui smiled politely which made Edward blush. Mui broke off the conversation abruptly and moved to set the small table careful of Emma's eyes that were lingering on the talkative duo.

Lunch went off smoothly as everyone enjoyed their light snacks with cake, sandwiches and biscuits. Mui looked at the sky which had started to turn grey. The sudden thundering was brushed aside by Captain Hill as mere passing, nothing to be worried about.

"Saab, we should go," Mui gathered the courage to speak as she knew the mountains, and such weather was never a good sign. Captain Hill's gaze frightened Mui as she held her tongue.His ego was definitely hurt, as a man in his position could never take order from a little girl.

"Go and pack the belongings. Don't just linger here," Elisa's sharp words were enough to move the tiny girl from her position. Mui reluctantly moved away from the sight of her employers, hurriedly gathering their belongings, worried that any time now there would be a downpour.

The Captain waited for the clouds to dissipate and the weather to become sunny again but the sky had been stubborn today as more grey clouds gathered, accompanied with loud thunders.

Mui looked at the sky, wishing for a better outcome than the one she was expecting. YOL camp was an hour away and even if they hurried, they still wouldn't reach back in time to steer clear of the rain. A few minutes later,the first few drops fell on the dry ground, engulfing the entire area in the aroma of fresh wet earth. Captain Hill was not one to accept his mistake and he pushed his wife and children to take shelter. They could only walk a few feet before falling prey to the rain, which by now was pouring hard, devouring even their meek cotton umbrellas. Elisa's dress was drenched and it had become difficult for her to walk with the weight of the wet dress.

"John, please wait. I can't go on like this," she pleaded as Captain Hill looked at his soaking wet wife who was now shivering with cold. He looked around trying to find shelter, catching a dilapidated broken bamboo shed. He pointed for everyone to move in the direction of the broken shed and everyone followed his lead.

The shed, made of thatched walls and a broken tin roof which was barely holding up, was their only hope as more and more people crammed the tiny space. Captain Hill instructed his soldiers to wait at one corner of the shed as he and his family occupied the other corner. The dingy shed leaked from several places but at least now they were away from the downpour. The minutes turned into hours with everyone just waiting for the rain to stop, but today it had decided not give up and be melodramatic. With the children squabbling, the chill in the air and the tiny space everyone was at the edge of their tolerance level.

Knowing that it might take a while, Captain Hill instructed the men to set up the table and chairs so that they could sit comfortably; the men sat on the cold floor of the shed. Edward, tired from the hustle bustle, strained to keep awake and drifted off to sleep in Elisa's arms. Mui sat crouched up on the floor, drifting off to interrupted sleep as her head tried to balance and find a good resting spot. After a while as the rain continued to show its might, even Captain gave up and slept on the increasingly uncomfortable chair.

Mui opened her eyes to the sunrays falling on her face from the holes in the roof. She looked around at the half sleepy half tired faces, all rising from their places and stretching to let their bodies ease the pain endured throughout the night. The shed seemed smaller to her than the night before as its contents were now more visible in the daylight.

Captain Hill instructed all the men to start moving back. Elisa also took the hint and woke up Edward and Emma. The journey back home was a silent one as no one knew the best possible subject to discuss. Edward who was usually very chirpy was too tired to even acknowledge the presence of people around him and pleaded to be carried which was forcefully declined.

On reaching her room, Mui was greeted by the very hungry Miti who was stunned by the sudden intrusion but still managed to wag his tale to welcome his owner.

"Oh my, I'm so sorry Miti. I forgot all about you. You must be hungry," she spoke softly brushing his soft fur. Miti licked her face with warmth still hoping to get something to eat as she moved him aside and left the room once again to get something for her dog. The guilt of leaving him alone and the sadness of being on an empty stomach were enough for her to forget her misery. She walked to Elisa's house.Carefully entering the kitchen so as to not disturb anyone in the house, she picked up two slices of bread.

"Who is that for? Are you stealing food?" Mui shaken by the sudden interruption, turned to find Emma standing at the door.

"No, I'm not stealing. Please."

Mui knew she could not convince Emma even if she wanted to, so she just held her head low and walked past Emma without another word.

"Where do you think you are going? I will tell mother what you have been doing," Emma warned her but by that time Mui had already walked out of the house, ignoring all the threats.

She gave Miti the piece of bread which he sedately ate, seemingly far from the wild animal he once was and now so tamed.

"What do I do Miti, I can't keep you here. Emma will tell Meemsaab and then she would throw you out on the street."

Tears rolled down her face as she hugged her pet who lovingly licked her tears. His big eyes trying to understand the pain of his owner, he broke from her embrace and comfortably sat on her lap, trying to soothe her.

"I can't keep you here," she uttered to Miti as if he understood. Her heart sank with every waking minute knowing that Elisa might just enter any moment. She looked at the lovable creature, calming herself down as she tried to find a solution to this unique problem.

"Yes, I know what we should do Miti." Finally she had come to a sordid conclusion, beaming at the satisfied answer.

She pulled the dog up from her lap and tying a rope around his neck, walked outside her room past the main gate towards the market. She looked around the market with many cluttered shops and saw Mohandas sitting in his little shop, smiling candidly at the familiar approaching young girl. The additional guest surprised him at first but then his eyes relaxed as he looked lovingly at the dog.

"Who is this little fellow?" he asked softly.

"He is Miti, and he needs a home. Uncle, can you please keep him with you? I would have taken care of him but I can't keep him there. I promise he would not bother you. He is very docile. See!" She spoke pointing towards the little dog.

"Oh child… Yes, I will keep him. Don't you worry about him," Mohandas rose, grabbing Miti's rope and pulling him towards his side.

Mui smiled at the kind hearted person she knew so well. "Thank you, Uncle. He is far from his family but maybe you can be his family!"

CHAPTER 10

URGE FOR FREEDOM

AUTUMN 1942

Elisa had kept a distance between the Mui and the children for a few months now, only allowing her to watch over the children.Mui had noticed that she had been on edge ever since Emma told her about Miti, any stress of home or even a slight disagreement with Captain Hill meant that Mui would have more unreasonable work. Elisa's nuisances had been so heavily loaded on Mui that she felt the brunt of it all on her tiny little shoulders.

Late autumn brought with it cold swift breeze. Mui felt the bitterness in the air coming from the partly closed window in her room. Luca had been kind enough to make her a floor rug which made her room a little warm. It was becoming colder by the day. She mustered the strength to leave her warm blanket and climbed atop the squeaking table, pushing her stone collection aside to close the window properly, as the shutters shuddered with the blowing wind. She tried moving the window panes but they stood fixated not ready to move from the defined position, when suddenly she heard screams mixed with sounds of rushing footsteps as a tall figure ran outside her window. She held her breath as the khaki uniformed man ran towards the boundary wall, trying to reach the top, leaping frantically to grasp the edge so that he could cross over.

He saw Mui staring at him through the window; noticing the desperation in his eyes accompanied by irrevocable strength as their eyes met for just a second. His face was covered in dirt with blood on the clothes. Shrieks from the officers' barracks reached her room, diverting the attention towards the door.

She turned her head quickly to face the prisoner again. He was running out of energy but his will was too strong to deter his wish for freedom. He turned away from the wall, looking for something that would help him to climb. He grabbed a big stone and put it steadily, leaning against the wall, stacking another stone on top of it but the stones were heavy and carrying each was taking its own time. He wearily managed to pile three, standing on the makeshift ladder, still falling short; he looked at his destiny.Warned of the consequence that would befall him; he dreadfully tried to level the border with all his strength. Not able to reach the edge he hesitatingly climbed down making the ill constructed structure fall beneath him as he fell to the ground on his knees and hands.

Mui gasped at such perseverance. "You will make it, try harder," she shouted from the window, managing to encourage him, petrified of the consequences. She turned and walked towards the door to help the man as British soldiers started coming in from all directions, one of them shoving her inside.

"Stay inside," he warned her.

She helplessly climbed back on juggler's brother which trembled with her weight, popping her head outside the window, nervous for the escapee.

Captain Hill marched with a band of troops right behind him with guns in their hands. Mui watched apprehensively as her stomach clenched with fear.

The height of the thick wall was too much for the prisoner and, with no plan in hand, he ran helter-skelter like a fanatical rabbit trying to find a hole he could hide in.

"Shoot!!" Captain Hill's voice roared with command as several rounds of bullets were fired by the British Indian soldiers - one piercing his heart; blood trickled down his khaki uniform and he fell to his knees taking in the final few gasps of life. Freedom was now in heaven as death clipped away his breath and he drifted away silently.

Mui had never seen death from so up close and the sight of blood was too much to stomach. She tried to find her voice but could not speak as crowds of people passed by her room.

Still atop the table, she tried to climb down as her legs trembled, even the juggler brother gave up and with a loud wham it came down, crumbling under the weight and she fell to the ground. She screeched with pain, mustering the courage to move her body from the floor. Finally giving up, she kept lying on the floor drifting away to sleep.

The sound of footsteps awoke the dainty soul, events of the shooting still fresh in her mind. She got up with an aching heart, looking at the window before finally deciding to go out, tenaciously trying not to look behind but before she knew it, her head had already turned as she took a fleeting glance at the wall.

Traces of blood still adorned the wall like fine art, and in the front was a stone slab where hours before a tall determined man had stood.

"Here lies the one who fell," Mui repeated to herself.

She quickly turned and went on to do her daily chores.

CHAPTER 11

WINTER 1942

A FRIEND IN NEED

Blooming of red roses marked the beginning of winter. Though the air had a bit of chill, it was adorned by the colourful hues of winter flowers, led by the army of red and pink roses. Captain Hill's prized possession, the garden, was well taken of under the watchful eye of Luca. It not just blossomed but flourished with health. Luca's visit was well anticipated by Mui who would stand looming over the garden waiting for his arrival which would be generally around noon so she would do the rest of her chores, leaving the drying of the clothes till the very end. Elisa's blissful ignorance towards their budding friendship was a blessing for both of them.

Mui woke up in the wintry air still feeling tired but managed to walk to the house which seemed quieter than usual, noticing that Emma was still in bed.

"Mui, Emma is not well; see that Edward goes to school on time," Elisa brushed aside Emma's hair to check her temperature.

"You stay in bed darling; I have to go but I will be back in no time. Take rest," Elisa kissed Emma's forehead and tucked her up in the blanket.

Mui went on to do as she was told. As noon approached she had almost finished her work, realising that she was late and not to miss the chance to see Luca she ran to the garden with a basket of washed clothes, hoping that he was still there.

"You late; I done," Luca smiled with a little sadness. His English vocabulary was far less as compared to that of Mui. But still he could manage to put across his point.

Mui nodded forlornly as she started hanging the clothes on the wire.

"Come, see." Luca struggled with the right words as Mui went closer to him.

"Rosa, rosa see…" Luca pointed to the gorgeous pink rose standing alone in all its beauty. Mui was genuinely awed by the beauty of the rose and Luca's enthusiasm as she shifted her gaze from him to the rose.

"Prendere… Uhhhh…" he scratched his head to find the right word. Making her laugh as he looked funny with one eyebrow searching the sky and one eye crinkling shut.

Unable to find the word, he just gave up and took his shears to cut the flower for Mui. The distraction of giving a gift disturbed Luca and he cut his finger, which bled heavily as he tried to hold it tight to stop the blood from draining. Mui stood in shock as the sight of blood made her nauseous.

"Oh, so much blood!" Mui could barely see due to the tears that blocked her view.

She quickly wiped her tears and rushed inside to get the first-aid kit, nearly knocking down Emma. Edward had once got a cut and she had seen Elisa clean his wound and bandage it. She scrambled through the kitchen cabinet and went out to Luca.

"Is fine," he tried consoling Mui who was now over powering him to settle down and let her take care of him. She gently cleaned the wound and bandaged it to perfection.

Luca was grateful for the help and picked up the rose which was lying on the floor, wiping the blood from it with his shirt.

"Thank you," Mui replied with affection.

"Next time cut just the rose please," she giggled.

"Yes," he replied laughing, leaving shortly after crossing Elisa on his way out.

In the urgency of the situation Mui had forgotten that Emma was in the house and she had almost knocked her down. Horrified about the outcome that would befall her, she stood at the corner of the garden giving Emma enough time to narrate her version of the incident to her mother. Walking slowly towards the house she clenched her stomach as she faced Elisa who looked appalled.

"How dare you!" she howled at Mui as Emma smirked with great satisfaction.

"That first aid is not for some raggedy prisoner! You have dishonoured the house, you ungrateful girl. Get out of here!" she raised her hand but calmed herself down, passing a disgusted look at her.

Mui held her head down and went to her room without any supper, her stomach rumbling with hunger. Over the last few months, Mui had become very pale and thin, unlike the girl who lived in the village.

She looked at the juggler brother which, after the last fall, had been repaired rather   amateurishly and was barely standing, her stone collection meticulously displayed on top. The lamp in the room flickered as she blinked her eyes and one by one each stone turned into a tiny living animal. Her eyes widened with amazement as she tried to catch the rabbit hopping frantically on the table.

"Come here you little fellow," she ran after the rabbit, unable to even reach it within catching distance.

A dog started barking making her ears ring, while a cat meowed all the way to her palm, gently purring. Little mice circled around her feet, nibbling on her toes softly as she shooed them away only to come back after a few minutes. Little birds flew across the room, chirping from one corner to the other, finally settling down on the window singing in their melodious voices.

Mui's body now swayed to the tune of the birds' song as she danced around the tiny room with mice, dog, cat, rabbit and a horse at her feet. A piece of cloth gently tangled her feet as she tripped and fell on the ground, waking up from the fantasy world. Her stone collection sat intact on the juggler's brother.

She walked back to her bed unable to sleep, tossing and turning with hunger. Her attention moved to the door as something stirred outside. Scared that it might be an animal or worse, a runaway prisoner, she gathered the courage to look outside her window which gave a very narrow view of the passage leading to the door. She peeped outside from the corner of the window only to find a hauntingly still passage.

"I'm sure I heard something," she thought as she walked towards the door with curiosity, opening the door ever so slightly to find a small packet wrapped in a dirty piece of cloth.

She cautiously picked up the packet wondering as to its contents and softly put it on the table.

"What could it be?"

Her patience had run out as she unwrapped the packet to find a portion of bread. She stood stiff in the stillness of the room, merely disturbed by the tears that trickled down her rosy cheeks. She took a bite from the bread, aware that it was the same kind that the prisoners ate.

CHAPTER 12

CIMA ITALIA, SPRING 1943

It was a bright sunny morning and Lavera looked surprisingly anxious that day to Angus's amusement. He loved it when Lavera was under the gun.

Lavera roamed around with a delicate yet quick pace and looked around the camp scavenging for troops that could accomplish the task at hand. He waved at some of the men to come to his side. When they were gathered, he passed on a series of instructions which most of them took in a confused state.

"Let me see what is going on there," said Angus to Luca, who looked disapprovingly bored as if Angus was walking in some sort of a trap.

Angus took his steps carefully towards a dishevelled Lavera who was now in a fit of rage mixed with confusion, trying to explain the technical work to illiterate slaves.

"Siete tutti bufali analfabeti, just get out and get me some real diligent people!"shouted Lavera.

Angus could not control his smile which was attentively noticed by Lavera.

"You are all smiles today. Let's see you climb the mountain; you start early morning tomorrow. Get five more people to come with you," remarked Lavera with satisfaction. He never liked Angus.

After the brief encounter, a set of instructions was given to Angus for mapping the mountain and getting back on time to report the findings. It was a common affair to send prisoners to map mountains for the British records as it helped them to keep track of the terrain. It was a dangerous affair as the mountains had dense forests; wild animals were ample and the terrain unpredictably unforgiving.

Angus, instead of being disheartened, seemed more relieved as the prospect of timed freedom was a cherished experience. He rounded four people along with Luca, who was dragged into the group, with promises of a day of liberty. He packed the flag of his country along with basic amenities with hopes of a great day.

Luca knew that several prisoners had done mapping and had come back with some body parts missing. Mui was the closest person Luca knew who had an idea about these mountains, better than anyone else. Luca walked around trying to catch a glimpse of her and when he finally saw her, he waved his hand frantically so that she noticed.

Although Mui had imparted all the terrain wisdom to Luca through the few words that they both could understand, and a mix of befuddling sign language, she was worried about the amateur travellers, aware of the harshness of the wilderness.

She lay awake at night anxious about Luca's destiny.

"They will get killed out there," she mumbled, worried.

The next morning was a particularly easy day. The children and Elisa were going out to the nearby town for a visit to Elisa's cousin and return the day after. She took the opportunity to sneak out of the camp at dawn. She knew Angus would have left for the expedition already so she hurriedly pursued the path they would have traversed, till she caught them at the foothills of the mountain.

Luca was surprised yet vexed with her, but knowing that she knew the mountain like the back of her hand appeased his nerves.

"Go back," he tried to dissuade her from coming.

"No," she said with a determination which could not he haltered.

Mui took command of the group, starting at the front of the pack guiding, directing and instructing the group as they traversed through the narrow ridges and small water streams. It was an uphill climb which had various rocky crossings. The climb started gradually but later the upward trek took toll on everyone's will Power.

Dhauladhar Mountains were very peaceful, mesmerising and enchanting yet dangerous. Angus noted down each and every obstacle, water stream, ridge and boulder that they encountered. After nine kilometres of uphill climb feet the air seemed thinner and Luca breathed heavily. Mui noticed this and signalled everyone to sit down for a few minutes to acclimatise. Luca's legs snivelled with cold and tiredness, as they had already climbed for almost four hours without any break.

In spite of Mui and Luca not speaking the same language they had this unspoken understanding that only they could decipher.

"Go go go…! It is time," gestured Mui, pointing her hands towards the sky, indicating that the sun would soon go down.

Mountains were home to various wild animals including leopards and panthers. The climb was slow and Angus was mesmerised by the spectacular steep gradient, meandering streams and smooth elevation.

The grassy path was bursting with broadleaf trees, pines and deodar trees with small patches of grass. They even saw a few shepherds grazing their flock of sheep on the rich grass there.

As they crossed the grassland they met with a small waterfall. Mui couldn't stop her excitement as she plunged her face in the tumbling water. The fresh water was enough to raise everyone's spirits. The closer they got to the top, the lesser the vegetation became till it almost disappeared.

"Arrrrrrrrrrrrrrrrrrrrrrrrrrrggggggggggggg!!" a loud shriek caught everyone's attention.

A large boulder had come loose and had come down tumbling on Angus's side. As he tried to shelter himself, he slipped and fell, almost cutting it too fine to the edge. Luca rushed to help his friend at the same speed with which Mui tried to stop him. Hilly areas are unpredictable and a few wrong moves could determine your fate.

"Stop!!!" shrieked Mui to everyone.

She signalled everyone to take shelter as one loose rock meant that more would fall in time.

Everyone gasped as they saw this tiny little girl move at a lightning speed and dictate everyone to safety. A few minutes' wait and they all were on their way again. It took them almost 6 hours to reach the top at 9350 feet.

They all glowed with happiness and shouted one another's names from the top.

They submitted the partly made Italian flag on top of the mountain and beamed with pride.

'Cima Italia, 1943,' everyone shouted in upheaving unison.

They could only spend some time on top as they had to reach back. Dark mountains were not a very friendly place to be. Mui was a silent spectator in all of this as she could only imbibe everyone's feelings. The journey back was a silent one with the stress and strain of the day's hard work piercing their fragile bodies.

Captain Hill didn't realise Mui was missing till late evening and searching for the girl was like a slap to his ego. He sent a few Indian soldiers looking for her but when none of them returned with her whereabouts, he assumed that she had run away to her home, and dismissed the matter from his mind.

Mui turned up late at night- dusty, muddy and extremely tired. Her petite long legs couldn't bear walking. She dragged her withered body over to her bed, fell flat on it and drifted into a dreamless slumber.

She woke up and saw Elisa next to her bed as she had missed her morning calls. Still half asleep from the tiring journey, Mui could not grasp the reality of the things happening around her.

Elisa shook her awake and slapped her face, turning the pale white skin to an apple red. Sharp pain awoke all her senses and tears filled her eyes.

Elisa left the room without saying a single word. Mui followed her back to the house, trying to get through the difficult day as her body ached in various places.

News of the successful climb had reached all nooks and corners of the camp. All prisoners, except Lavera, celebrated. He was disappointed by Angus' return.

Colours of white, blue and red decorated each barrack and patriotic songs were sung by the prisoners.

The zeal was so high that the captives forgot that they were mere prisoners. With each rising pitch, Captain Hill's tolerance was tested.

Prisoners, blissfully unaware of the ramifications, sang with high spirits, and one of them joined in with a flute made from the local bamboo. He played wonderfully with soft music notes in between each pause. The music from the flute mesmerised the awestruck audience which was completely silent,listening to the palpitating notes.

Captain Hill had reached his limit and the unified singing, accompanied by the music, pushed him over the edge. He grabbed his rifle and flung it across his shoulder, moving with piqued steps towards the prisoners' barracks. Two more soldiers joined their commander on the quest for silenceas he marched swiftly to the barrack where all the commotion was going on.

"Si videil Piaverigonfiar le sponde, e come ifanticombattevan l'onde"others sang to the sound of flute as the melodious music echoed in the barrack while numerous eyes watched spellbound.

Captain Hill cut through the dumbstruck audience, making his way towards the centre of attention. He took out his rifle and in one brisk shot, hit the prisoner as blood splattered all over the tiny space. He turned arrogantly and walked back shoving aside the stunned crowd who stood rooted to the ground, unable to move or even voice their disbelief.

"He was just singing," Angus shook with incredulity looking at the blood covered body, flute still in the palm of his hand.

"We need to bury him," Lavera's voice trembled as he spoke. His command was followed wordlessly as another grave stone was erected among the others.

That night everyone stood in silence, even Lavera shaken up by the incident.

LATE SUMMER, 1943

Luca spent hours staring intermittently at the towering boundary wall while gardening. This upset Mui as she worried about the state of his mind aware of the flute incidence.

"Don't think about it," she uttered leaving him to do his work. She went to look after Edward, hoping that time would pass quickly and she could go back home with her aunt, who was due any minute.

Light showers in the summer had painted rainbows in the sky. From the window of his house, Edward saw the droplets falling from the sky and he ran to the garden trying to fruitlessly catch one of them in his tiny little hands.

"Don't jump in water Edward," Mui pleaded watching him enjoy the drizzle. He was not the one to listen today as he dragged her along to enjoy the rain. Luca watched her forget everything and just be a child, splashing, jumping and playing in the rain, drenched from top to bottom.

Mario and Antonio's faces flashed in front of his eyes watching the children play. A sad smile swept across his face trying to gather the mere memory of his children. He got up to leave and noticed Emma in the window, staring enviously at them.

"Mui careful," he warned her but in vain, as she was too engrossed in play. Panic gripped him when he saw Elisa walking towards them; he grabbed Mui and jolted her to reality.

Scared of the sudden shock she looked at him and then at the approaching duo.

"You filthy little girl! Look at you, all covered in dirt. Go inside Edward!" Elisa roared with anger.

"If you like the muck so much stay here!" she continued, commanding her to stay put till the time she relieved her. Luca stood in horrified silence watching his little friend get punished.

"She is just a little girl," he whispered catching Elisa's ears who turned her attention towards the scruffy prisoner.

"You should be glad that it is me standing here and not my husband. Leave now," she ordered as Luca hung his head and left, helplessly watching Mui standing in dirt. Never had he felt so Powerless towards the British regime than that day.

Elisa left Mui to ponder on her mistakes and amend them in the most polished way possible. Dark clouds gathered in the sky as cold winds started blowing, making the weather a wee bit colder. The rain had drenched Mui's clothes. She shivered and tried to cuddle up to get warm.

After sometime in the rain, her punishment was over as Elisa concluded that she had learnt her lesson.

Mui dragged her cold shivering body to the room, water still dripping from clothes. She fell on the floor unconscious, drained of all the energy, only to be woken up by Vati who held her head in her lap, tenderly caressing her hair.

"You are not well Malini. I will stay here with you today; tomorrow we will go home. Take rest child," she kissed her forehead and fed her supper.

"Don't worry about Meemsaab. I have spoken to her and taken her permission," her words put the anxious girl to peace.

Their conversation was interrupted by a peeping face which brought both of them to their feet.

"Who is it?" Mui spoke.

"Edward," came the innocent voice from the door.

"Oh my, what are you doing here Edward? Please go back home," Vati let him in only to instruct him to go back, since it was already too late. If Elisa noticed his absence, everyone would be in trouble.

"I'm sorry Mui," he said, passing a bright violet flower in her hand.

"It's alright Edward. Now please go back home. You should not be out so late," Mui smiled affectionately at him while Vati escorted him back home.

"At least you have one friend here Malini," Vati exclaimed.

"Aunty, I have many."

CHAPTER 13

AUTUMN 1943

STRANGER'S LOVE

Strong winds blew the pale leaves on the road, covering the entire camp in dried leaves while the hues of fall rapidly spread across. Mui's dress swept up in the blowing wind. She held onto her clothes, swiftly moving towards the house. The wind made it a little difficult to walk. She looked up at the gate visible in the distance, but the house still remained a few meters further.

This trip to the market was particularly worrisome to her as she could not see Miti or Mohandas. His shop had remained closed for almost a week now without any intimation to Mui and this worried her.

"What happened child?" Mui turned to notice an old woman sitting on a large stone at the side of the road. Her wrinkly face reflected her wisdom and her eyes had such sorrow that only a great loss could bring. Her soft affectionate words were enough to lure Mui into close proximity of the stranger, as the old woman looked on with great love.

"Go on child," she encouraged the little girl to speak up.

"I'm so worried. I don't know where they could have gone." Mui burst out crying as the anxiety that gripped her now seemed too real to ignore.

"Who are you talking about child? Where is your family?" The old woman enquired softly.

"Mohandas uncle. He owns a cloth shop in the bazaar. I work at the camp and mother lives in Thunksa village" Mui managed to put the answer together, shaking a little from the sudden surge of emotions.

"Is that right? Mohandas?" The old woman was persistent in her enquiries as Mui looked at her with a grim face.

Mui noticed the elegance of her stance, the folds of her maroon saree with a thin golden border, the baggy eyes and the neatness of her plaited hair. She didn't look like a woman who would sit on a stone next to the road. Mui gave her a perplexed look. This made her conscious of the horde of questions she was throwing at such a confused child.

"I am Sudha," she smiled while getting Mui's name in response.

"Well Mui, are you hungry?"she could make out the thin body and the deprived eyes.

"Yes," Mui replied with caution but the kindness in her voice added to the trust that Mui could not deny.

"I had made food, see. I am too old to eat so much; will you please eat with me?"

She opened a small metal tiffin box which had three rotis with some cooked vegetables. The aroma of the food was captivating as Mui drifted closer to the food. The old lady handed over a roti as the wind tried to blow it away from her hand.

"We better shift under some roof," she nudged Mui to move to the empty shed nearby and take shelter from the howling wind and eat in peace.

Mui relished the home cooked meal that she craved every now and then. Though there was not much, still the old lady gave most of it to Mui, barely eating one roti herself. She watched as Mui gobbled up the roti and delectable vegetables with delight.

"I hope you liked it," Sudha said watching Mui eat. The little one was so busy eating she didn't hear it the first time. The second time Sudha asked, she just looked up with her mouth full and nodded with happiness.

"Thank you, aunty," Mui said after wiping her face on the sleeve of her shirt.

"Aunty, if you don't eat so much food, then why do you even make so much?" Realisation had just hit Mui as she looked at the old weary woman.

Sudha was taken aback by the sudden candidness of the child, the question had brought back all the warped memories that she had tried so hard to forget.

"I always make for two people Mui. Me and my son," she smiled meekly, knowing positively the next question.

"Oh, I am sorry.Did I eat your son's share?" Mui felt embarrassed. She knew she should have asked this before throwing everything down her throat.

"No child, I am glad you ate. My son is dead." The pain in her trembling voice took Mui by surprise. She backed away two steps, unsure of what to say. She stood there staring at the lady, who now seemed more than a stranger.

"Do you miss him?" were the only words that came out of Mui's mouth and she regretted them the moment she said them.

"Every day," she said as tears shinned in her tired eyes. "One day I will meet him in heaven and we will have each other again," she shrugged her tears away and smiled politely at the little girl.

The sound of the breeze was the only thing that broke the silence as both of them stood there looking into each other's eyes.

"Sorry, I wanted to tell you that I had heard some shopkeepers saying that a few shopkeepers had gone to the mountain top temple to ask for peace. I wanted to tell you then only but you were so befuddled. Hope it helps you," Sudha smiled gently.

"Yes, thank you so much."

This news had uplifted Mui's spirits. She bid goodbye to her rescuer and carried on towards the house with a full stomach and a calm mind.

Mui looked back at the shelter but could not locate Sudha. In the next few days she tried to look for her but could never find her. Even when Mohandas came, he could not identify such a woman.

Mui thought of her as her angel and kept the story of meeting her close to her heart.

CHAPTER 14

WINTER, 1943

THE DOLL

Captain Hill had gone to painful lengths to get the valued gift asked by Emma on her ninth birthday. Emma excitedly opened the hefty present, which was almost half as tall as her, neatly wrapped in red coloured paper with a golden bow on top.

There lay a beguilingly exquisite doll wearing a pink laced frock and white sandals. It had beautiful golden locks that fell to her shoulders and eyes as blue as the sea.

"See how tall she is Mother! She is so beautiful, thank you, thank you, thank you" squeaked Emma with excitement.

Edward just sat admiring the rare beauty of the toy. Elisa and Hill looked pleasantly content with the delight the doll had brought.

Mui had never seen a real doll in her life, all she knew were the rags that her aunt had sewn to make her a temporary doll on her fifth birthday. She sat admiring the toy, looking at it with longing eyes. The day was full of the hustle bustle of the birthday party, with cake, food, music and children playing around as Mui watched.

The house work took the rest of the day and while the children were put to bed, Mui still had loads to do. While cleaning the main hall she saw Emma's doll lying on a chair alone, seemingly sad.

"You look alone, do you want company?" Mui picked up the delicate doll and cuddled her with warmth and love.

"I will sing you a song so that you sleep peacefully tonight," she sang a melodious song for the little doll, while she completed her final load of work. She carried the doll back to her bed, fearing that she would feel frightened if left alone. She wrapped herself up in blanket along with the peaceful doll lying next to her, drifting off to sleep.

Mui awoke to Emma's loud shrieks as she hustled up and ran to her room.

"My doll mother, it's missing!" Emma wailed, as Elisa desperately tried to console the child. Edward, puzzled by the situation in front of him, started crying in confusion. Elisa was befuddled with two children crying inconsolably.

Mui ran to the room looking perplexed at the situation, eventually realizing that the doll lay neatly on her bed. The trouble of the situation had not occurred to her before.

"I... Ha... Ha... Have the doll meemsaab; she was alone so I thought she would get frightened and I took her to sleep with me."

Elisa looked relieved at first but anger got the better of her as she slapped Mui across her face. The jolt was so forceful that Mui fell on the ground, her head buzzing with pain.

"Go to your room and don't ever steal things. Return the doll at once!" exclaimed Elisa with authority. Emma and Edward kept silent and then followed their mother out of the room leaving Mui alone to cry in silence.

Mui managed a few sobs before going to complete her daily chores. She went outside carrying the basket of washed laundry and found Luca entering the garden looking around for her. Her eyes shimmered with tears and a forlorn expression which was conspicuously evident to Luca, making him worried. He crawled cautiously next to her, gave her a loving gaze and to his surprise she burst out crying. He held her close to him and patted her head so as to understand the reason for this solemn mood. In her own words and using gestures, Mui expressed the tale of the lost doll which made Luca envious of the people living in a free world.

"Do not worry about it," he consoled affectionately as he wiped away her tears. He was the friend she needed and just having him close was enough to give her the strength. That day she saw her friend trim the hedge precariously aware that he was keeping an eye on her too. Luca went back with a heavy heart, sharing the details with Angus and knowing that there was little they could do.

"Maybe we can do something," said Angus.

Luca was now hopeful. Over the years Angus had formed various bonds which benefitted him in the oddest way possible. His ingenuity was well known and he had become one of the most resourceful prisoners in the camp.

In a matter of days, he managed to convince the carpenter to carve a wooden doll, the tailor to stitch a dress for the doll using rags and the painter to paint the doll's eyes and mouth. The stunning, carved doll had black painted hair, beautiful big black eyes, rosy cheeks and a gorgeous khaki frock. Angus gave it to Luca, who was touched by the gesture and the crafting ability of his friend. He wrapped the doll in paper and waited for the right time to give it to Mui.

The days went by quietly after that with children in school, Mui tending to the housework and the frequent visits from Luca, which she always looked forward to. Luca was finding it hard to give the doll to Mui as she was always running around with some work. Catching her to give a doll and not get accused of stealing again was a tricky thing to do.

One morning while trimming the hedge he saw the opportunity to sneak into her room and keep the doll on the bed. Excitement filled his soul at the thought of Mui's beaming face.

Mui had a tough day and just wanted some peace in her room. She sat on her bed unaware of the packet at first but as she moved to lie down the packet slipped and fell to the ground catching her attention.

"What is this?" she bent to pick up the packet. Careful of its contents, she gently unfurl it

and was astonished to find a well-crafted doll; tears welled up as she picked up the toy, examining it from side to side in disbelief, as if she was in her dream world. She jolted herself to wake up from the fantasy world to still find the beautiful doll in her hands.

"It's real, the doll is real!"

Her eyes widened with delight as she hugged and cuddled the toy, placing it next to her pillow as she fell asleep looking in the deep blue eyes of the doll.

That night Luca slept peacefully, content with the thought of bringing joy to a small girl who was in desperate need of some magic.

CHAPTER 15

SPRING 1944, A LOST SOUL

Vati's absence for the past two months, accompanied with the urge to meet her mother, worried Mui. But she silently bore the stress, patiently waiting for her aunt to turn up one day so that she could go and see her mother- not only because she was unwell but also because the changes in her surroundings worried her. Constant marches and protests were a common sight. The demand for an independent country was catching up faster than she knew. Even Mohandas had joined the rebellion, though she couldn't understand the need for the non-violent marches but she did understand freedom.

Day by day the non-violent marches became a twinge for Captain Hill as he tried to deter them but to no avail. Mahatma Gandhi's name and his slogans were sung in unison among the Indian crowd, which were nervously ignored by him. The urgent summons to Dilli by British command didn't come as a surprise to him. He had been aware of the surrender by Italy to the Allied Forces and the fortification of the freedom movement in India. Elisa, shaken up by the drastic changes that were occurring around her, prepared herself for the unforeseen future.

Captain Hill's departure brought with it an uncomfortable rein on Elisa who now restricted herself to the walls of her house, even limiting the movements of her children. Mui drowned herself in work, partly able to grasp the gravity of the situation which was quite evident on everyone's face including Luca's, who seemed pleased by all this.

"Your aunt hasn't come here in sometime. Do you need to go home?" Elisa's words took Mui by surprise as the sudden empathy was never expected from her.

"Yes" Mui replied meekly.

"Will you be able to go home alone?"

Mui nodded which was acknowledged as a yes by Elisa.

"Then go tomorrow and be back by evening; also take your earnings and give them to your aunt," she continued.

The next morning Mui took the long road home to meet with her mother. By the time she reached Thunksa village it was already noon. Her dreary looking tiny home was visible as she passed through the village to reach her home, conscious of the concerned looks coming her way. She looked at herself wondering the reason for being the centre of attention.Her sluggish steps turned to a rapid pace, trying to get through the gawking eyes.

"What are you doing here?" Vati spoke with a tremble.

"Why haven't you come? I kept waiting for you!" fumed Mui, pushing her aside to enter the house.

The sight of her ailing fading mother was too much to bear as she collapsed on the floor trying to catch her breath. The roll of money fell from her pocket, scattering all over the floor.

"Malini," Vati spoke tenderly, pulling her up from the ground and gently wrapping her arms around her.

"Ma!" Mui shrugged herself free from the embrace to go near her mother. Aisama turned slowly to look at her daughter, staring miserably at her.

"Mui," pain accompanied the soothing words coming out of her lips. She grabbed Mui's hand affectionately and kept holding on to it. Mui lay awake at night lying next to her mother, holding her warm hand lovingly, till it started to turn cold.

"Aunty," Mui spoke, dreading the worse as Vati got up from the rolled- up bed. She crept near her sister, feeling her pulse; Mui's curious eyes did not shift an inch from her mother.

Vati hung her head low, giving a devastating look to Mui who just stood silent, unable to take in the reality. Aisama lay flat on her bed, her tender loving face still unbroken. Mui sat next to her bed holding the delicate hand for the last time.

Vati kept her hand on her shoulder trying to console the little soul, but Mui couldn't believe her fate and fell to the ground as tears rolled down her eyes accompanied with incumbent soft sobs. Vati pulled her up encasing her in a warm affectionate hug.

Both walked out of the house in silence, the realisation of Aisama's death settling clearly in Mui's mind. A few steps away from her house seemed like a miles walk and Mui's feet felt heavy with remorse. As the minutes ticked away, the news travelled the length and breadth of the village; people started gathering outside their house to pay condolences. Pratap came in a hurry along with the children.

"It was as if she was just waiting for Malini to come," Vati spoke softly in Pratap's ear as he nodded in agreement. He walked towards the little girl with a heavy heart.

"Mui, we are there for you child," his words had so much warmth that they hit Mui the hardest. She broke down and burst into a river of tears, crying loudly for her mother.

"Ma....," she kept repeating over and over again until Vati held her in her arms to console her. Pratap went inside the house as it was time to lay Aisama to rest. He took the body out. Mui gave her mother a final kiss, parting with a smiling image of her mother in her mind. She seemed stronger than the frail girl Vati had known all her life.

"Don't worry Malini. We are here for you. If you want, you can come and live with us; we will make do," Vati spoke intermittently, trying to phrase the right sentence. Affection was not her forte but those words touched Mui.

"I have to go back," Mui spoke with determination, looking into her aunt's sad eyes. She composed herself, wiped her tears and got up, ready to leave.

"But...," Vati was cut short by the little girl's hurried egress from the house.

"Leave her, she needs time," Pratap said, holding Vati's hand to stop her from going after Mui.

Mui walked the lonely road to the camp with memories of her mother etched in every part of her mind. It all felt like a dream to her, hoping that she would wake up any moment by Elisa's calls.

***

Mohandas was in a good mood today as he walked towards the camp with an order that he was delivering by hand. He saw Mui walk past him with no semblance of life in her form, her head hung low, and her feet seeming to drag her body.

"Mui," he walked closer to her, perplexed by the situation. She was caught off guard by the sudden intrusion in her privacy as she looked up at the familiar plump face.

"Mother died. My heart aches, will it ever be alright?" Mui's innocent words pieced his heart as nothing could mend a broken heart.

"You will be alright child; time heals all wounds," he spoke from wise experiences of his past. He accompanied her till the house, watching her anxiously as she went inside the door.

Mui walked inside to find Elisa sitting in the rocking chair, looking out of the window as her hands crocheted a beautiful pattern. The sound from the chair irked Mui's ears as she moved closer to Elisa.

The hushed footsteps caught Elisa's attention and she turned her head to look at the frail girl, who stopped a few feet away from her.

"She died!"

Elisa's hands stopped weaving while the hook fell on her lap at the abrupt news. She looked at Mui with an

affectionate gaze, moving towards her. She stood as close to her as comfortable and kept her hand on her head, stroking it gently.
"It will be alright dear."

CHAPTER 16

FREEDOM

EARLY SUMMER, 1944

The freedom movement was spreading rapidly across British India. YOL camp was also getting affected by the same people who were demanding a free republic. Captain Hill was not impervious to the situation but there was little he could do to stop it; so he handled it the best way he knew- by making the life of the prisoners miserable.

The trips to environs were prohibited and all leisure activities were suspended as he tightened his grasp on the prisoners.

The death of another prisoner at the hands of Captain Hill fuelled the burning fires of revolt among the prisoners; even Lavera was affected by the sudden change.

"Till when will we obey the commands thrown at us, tiricordipersinol'Italia o ancheituoifratellichesonomorti," Angus spoke exasperated.

"How many will fall for the lost cause of freedom or even dreams of a free life, Luca? We need to do something. This prison isn't home!" he continued.

"Angus, sembrache la liberta mi stiasfuggendo dale dita. What can we do?" Luca was a practical man and the Powerlessness of the situation was not new to him.

"You sit and ponder about your freedom Luca, I will make sure we all remember our brothers in arms."

Angus's fortitude and determination were beyond Luca's understanding. He saw him pull up a stone used for building houses, and place it on the ground as a foundation stone of the structure that he had been planning to erect for a long time. Many prisoners, along with Luca, joined the cause as stone upon stone was gathered to erect the monument.

Round stones were placed at the bottom with gaps between them. They were covered on top with black slates. After three layers Angus paused to think about the best way to express the emotion in everyone's heart through the structure.

He looked at all the helping hands and placed three stones on top, the centre stone held between two slates in the shape of V. Everything was held together by the weight of the stones and the balance of the structure. The erected memorial made entirely of slates and stones,wonderfully portrayed the wings of a bird, struggling so that it could be free from captivity.

"Orahailibertafratellimiei" Angus spoke, as he looked at the crowd around him, nodding his head for everyone to pay their respects to the lost brothers.

The new structure had caused a stir in the camp and everyone curious enough was there to see it. Mui saw it from a distance but was unable to understand the meaning of it all. Captain Hill dismissed the memorial as inconsequential as compared to the rebellion rallies outside the camp. Walking back to the garden, Mui saw Luca purge away the weeds and she ran towards him to clear her mind.

"Luca what is that structure?"

Luca shifted his attention from the cunning weeds to the curious little girl.

"It's a memorial for our brothers Mui, who we have lost in the attempt to attain freedom."

Mui's eyes widened at the idea of freedom but a doubt still lingered in her mind.

"But you have everything here Luca, making it so comfortable. Then why crave freedom?"

Luca was taken aback by the sheer innocence of the girl. Mui was always astounded by all the comforts that the prisoners had which seemed far more than what she had-books, library, theatre were all luxuries for them to indulge in.

"A day of freedom is more desirable than any day of comforts," replied Luca, almost sad.

Mui couldn't understand his words that day, but they occupied her heart for a long time. Luca left Mui to carry on with her work, until the next time they met. A few days passed without any aggravations from Captain Hill, the prisoners or the local freedom fighters as the season changed from the summer sun to the mild rains.

Rain made the entire camp damp yet delightfully, the air smelled of wet earth. The nip in the air was surprisingly pleasant as everyone wanted to just cuddle up in a blanket, enjoying the falling drops. Wet ground always made Mui want to eat dirt, more embarrassing was that she relished it.

Elisa disliked the rains, especially here, as it would rain incessantly for days making everything difficult- clothes would not dry, the house would always seem dirty, the garden couldn't be maintained and the children were cooped up inside, driving her insane.

To Mui, she seemed so much on edge that half the day she would spend trying to avoid contact. It was a particularly tough day as Elisa had dinner guests coming in. Her dress needed some sewing to repair a visible tear that she had just noticed. She asked Mui to repair the damage and bring it in as soon as she was finished. The occasional dinners were a family tradition and Elisa loved to host such lavish suppers with fine wine and exotic food. She was gracious and groomed for the day.Her elegance even showed through her clothes, which were the finest ones she had.

Mui dragged the white and pink striped gown out to the main hall; it was such a long dress that it dangled mostly on the floor, drowning Mui in it.

She sat down admiring the fabric of the dress, running her hands through the silky soft cloth. The small tear was barely visible in the folds of the dress but she knew her meemsaab was very meticulous and such a small thing would not go unnoticed. She gently and carefully sewed the tear, so perfectly done that it seemed to have never been there. She examined the stitch to make sure it was good enough and then went to Elisa's room, pretty content with her work.

It took Elisa a few moments to scrutinize the dress, and then she noticed the bottom which was covered with dirt. "What happened to the bottom? It's all muddy. Mui what do you think I will wear in the evening?" Elisa spoke, horrified. She was so annoyed that her temper got the better of her and she pushed Mui out of the house and into the pouring rain.

"You will stay here until I tell you to go to your room, you are such an ungrateful child," barked Elisa with such ferocity that Mui had never seen before, tears welling up in her eyes.

Mui stood in the torrential downpour, drenched to the core and shaking miserably with cold. Even her tears were getting smeared down by the rain; but there was no mercy and it shook every bone in her body. Mui was out for almost half hour when she started feeling dizzy and fainted on the ground,falling with a loud thump.

The next thing she recalled was someone carrying her icy body to her room and wrapping her in blankets. The distorted image of a tall man still lingered in her mind as her eyes wandered into the dream world.

Luca sat with his friend till she warmed up and then sneaked out and into his barrack as Angus covered his absence.

"She is as cold as this rain Angus; I wish freedom was a choice for both of us,"murmured Luca in a disheartened tone.

STONE RELIC

The rather uncommon stone relic was made by the Italian prisoners housed in the YOL PSW camp from 1941 to 1945. The topmost pair of stones are symbolic of man's unsatisfied thirst for freedom depicted here as a pair of wings of a bird struggling to free itself from captivity. The rest of the structure represents prison walls. This beautiful idea enshrines the tribute which this band of Italians, although captives, left behind as an emblem of the human spirit, to uphold and emulate for posterity.

To this day it stands undisturbed by the fellow soldiers and even by the unforgiving fury of both nature and time.

CHAPTER 17

AUTUMN, 1944

THE SHIFT

It had been ages since Mui had seen Miti and it seemed just the right time to go visit him. Playing with the money in her hand, she crossed the narrow street of the crowded market, bought the customary biscuits and came prancing to Mohandas' shop, noticing the now very healthy Miti sitting politely next to him. Even before Mohandas could lay his eyes on Mui, Miti started jumping up and down, his long snout hovering in mid-air trying to smell the air and continuously wagging his tail as if some ghost had entered his body. Mohandas yanked his chain to calm him down, wondering about the sudden excitement in him. As soon as Mui came within visible distance, he applied his entire force on the chain, dragging Mohandas behind him as he lovingly climbed on top of Mui, inadvertently knocking her down.

"Down Miti, down" yelled Mohandas trying to pull him back with all his Power, making his huge round belly wobble profusely. After a short tete-a-tete with his old friend, Miti had calmed down enough to move aside and pull herself up from the floor.

Mui couldn't stop laughing as the inexorable licks from her old friend, accompanied by Mohandas's squeaks, made it all a humorous situation. Even after Mohandas had managed to pull Miti away his belly still wobbled like jelly, making Mui's eyes tear up trying to control her laugh. She looked at her dress trying move her eyes away from the dishevelled looking uncle.

"What have you been feeding him uncle?" Mui laughed a little, while dusting the dirt off her dress.

"It's nice to see you here Mui. I wasn't expecting you any time soon, knowing about all the commotion that is happening around here." Mui raised an eyebrow at that remark, not sure as to the reason behind so many disturbances.

"Uncle, what is happening?"

 She looked at him hoping to get an honest reply. The atmosphere changed drastically while Mohandas tried to find the right words to explain things to a little child. Mui got quieter which did not help with the silence that had already taken over the shop. Even Miti looked lazily at both of them as he finally settled down and went to sleep near Mui's shoes.

"I don't know child. Maybe you are too small to understand it all," he tried to let her down gently.

"I'm eleven, Uncle. Please don't let my age be a hindrance to the fact that I'm going to get affected by the future, whether you tell me or not. It is better to be prepared for what is coming," Mui spoke diligently.

"Hmmmmm," Mohandas was surprised how wise the little girl, who just a few years ago seemed so timid and helpless, had become.

"The freedom movement is heating up Mui. Rebel forces and the non-violence movements across the country have spread like wild fire. Rumours are circulating that the time is near when the British will be pushed out of the country. We might have a sovereign country; Baapuji has said he will get us freedom. Be careful child, no one goes down without a fight."

His fervent words ruffled Mui's peace. She looked at him horrified, unable to grasp the complexity of the situation.

"Uncle!" only one word escaped her lips as she heaved a heavy sigh.

"Go home Mui, non-violence can sometimes stir violence if kept inside for too long. I want you to be safe."

He looked at Mui with worried eyes as she half-heartedly left for the camp.

Walking along the path, she now started noticing the little things that she had ignored in the past. New faces had not come in for a while and even the older ones seemed to vanish out of sight one by one. Barracks seemed wearier than usual, low groans of the condemned prisoners had tapered to occasional whimpers. Even Captain Hill seemed distracted all the time; Elisa seemed jittery and the children were more polite than usual.

She halted to acknowledge Luca performing his daily ritual in the garden.

"Luca what is happening?" She said in a low voice, her watery eyes looking perturbed by the realisation of the facts around her.

"I'm not sure Mui. Lavera has been quite secretive about something. But I think they are moving us to some other place," Luca could never lie to his friend.

"What! But..." she paused for a minute, then decided to leave it at that,and sat next to her friend as he trimmed the hedges.

Mui looked at Luca with a horrified expression as a sinking feeling in the pit of her stomach gripped her. Tears welled up in her eyes as she gathered the fallen autumn leaves.

"No child, you be strong. Cry all you want with me, but after I go, I don't want you to shed a tear." Luca had a way of providing comfort.

Mui looked up and gave in to tears as she struggled to catch her breath in between loud sobs. Luca gripped her tight and let her head rest on his chest, holding her with all the comfort he could give.

"There, there, it will be ok. You will be ok; you are stronger than this," he said stroking her long dark brown hair.

"I...I can't...I.... Can't.... Stop.... Crying...,"Mui repeated in between sobs.

Luca looked around and lightly released Mui from his grip till she stood alone, confused by the sudden separation. Luca moved swiftly as if he had some agenda

on his mind, looking through all the flowers in the garden, finally focusing on a small vibrant marigold flower. He plucked it softly and brought it back to Mui.
"Alla bambina che e diventataamica(to the little girl who became a friend)," he said offering the flower.She took it and held it in her hands, not able to understand the words that were spoken but getting the emotion that was meant.

CHAPTER 18

WINTER 1944

GOODBYES

Autumn had passed silently with very little disturbance. The quiet all around pierced like needles, as if something big was coming soon.

Luca and Mui had been preparing for the worst in the past few months. As the new season settled in, there came a new hope that things might not change and the calm was there to stay. The strong winter winds made everyone wrap themselves up in woollens that they had stored away.

Luca felt the nip in the air as he held his clothes tighter, warmly wrapping himself with the stole that had jagged edges. It was oddly made as the knitting was of a rookie but he loved it since it was gifted to him by the one person he loved the most, Mui. He was astonished that an eleven year old child could understand a thirty year old man with a maturity that was even hard to find in people older than him. He wandered around with a lost expression and an unfazed will to do something for his little friend.Hushed rumours were coming from all nooks and corners of the camp about India's struggle for freedom which had taken a high pace throughout the country.It put a question mark on the certainty of his stay, making him more worried about her now than ever. Many stories of the freedom fighters were coming every day.This made Mui excited as she revelled in the heroic tales of the freedom fighters sacrificing their lives for a free country; but they troubled Luca.

According to Lavera, Britain had lost miserably in the war, and with India's push for freedom their future seemed to hang in the balance. Luca and Angus nervously waited for the day when their fates would be decided.

A few days passed without any real news. There were some conjured-up versions of the sadistic prisoners who sought pleasure in others' miseries. Fake lists would appear and disappear in a matter of seconds, even shaking Lavera's faith once in a while; but unlike most of the other prisoners, he was sure that he would be well taken care of; maybe even taken with one of the officers to their country. False hopes and perturbed beliefs were commonly lurking in the hearts of all prisoners. Even the British seemed fazed by the same. There was an inbound current in the camp that everyone could feel.

"Something is going on Luca," Angus said anxiously. Luca's eyes were fixated on the petals which glimmered like pearls as the noon light fell on the dew drops. The weather was cloudy but a few sunrays managed to escape and make their way to the ground below.

"Luca! Listen to me..." Angus was cut short as he noticed Captain Hill making his way towards the barracks. Luca's concentration was broken with a strong nudge from his friend, bringing him back to the real world.

"What is he doing here?" Angus spoke confused at the turn of events. Hill was rarely seen roaming around the likes of these prisoners that he detested so much, yet who had been put under his care.

Captain Hill made his way to the prisoners' barracks with a very determined look on his face, seeming disturbed by the turn of events. He stood in the centre of the ground and waited for a few minutes till he was encircled by the inquisitive prisoners. Lavera pushed everyone aside and moved to the front row making sure he did not miss anything.

"What can we do for you sir? Did we do something wrong?" Lavera's words annoyed most of the prisoners.

"Idiota! He is always trying to please them as if they are going to miss him," Angus was never the one to hold onto his feelings. Better out than in, he would say.

Luca shrugged to divert his attention from his extensively verbose friend to Captain Hill. Luca towered over everyone, easily able to see everything even when standing at the back of the crowd, while this was another complaint by Angus who was much shorter and struggled to see through the crowd.

Captain Hill stood taut and spoke in a very firm and cold voice, not letting anyone in on his true feelings. He stood with piercing cold eyes and cleared his throat as if trying to find the least amount of words that would make sense. "Starting from today you will all be divided into two groups, one will be sent to South Africa and the other to Australia. Pack your belongings as we will start sending you in groups from tomorrow. You will march to Kangra station at the break of daylight." These words spread like wild fire among all the prisoners. Lavera hushed his anxious brothers in arms, trying to maintain his inner calm while uproar broke out.

There were loud voices as confused prisoners were trying to understand the situation while Lavera tried to hush everyone down.

"Staicalmo, amici miei, niente di cui preoccuparsi.Saremo ben curati(Keep calm my friends, nothing to worry about. We will be well taken care of)." Lavera's words were falling on deaf ears but he paid no heed to the cries and kept enforcing his version on everyone.

Captain Hill gave Lavera a cautionary look and left abruptly, without a second word or any explanation as to what was happening.This was too much to ask from an officer who had no affiliation to the prisoners he had spent a few years with. Lavera ran behind him but was gestured to return to the barracks; his face dropped with the cold treatment but he obeyed, walking miserably back to his barrack, disturbed by the new occurrence and his lost fate.

British soldiers disseminated all over the barracks, instructing all prisoners to move towards their spaces.

"Where do you think you are pushing me to? I command the prisoners!" Lavera's unrealistic optimism was undeniable. He collapsed at the gate of his barrack as a soldier tried to push his heavy rotund body in.

Luca and Angus gave each other worried looks as all of them were shoved into their barracks like a herd of cattle. "I knew this was coming," Angus' tone was subdued as he was waiting for this day to come.

Angus, along with all the other prisoners, packed the little belongings they had while Luca swiftly moved past everyone and went outside looking for Mui.

CHAPTER 19

THE FINAL GOODBYE

Mui could sense a different air in the camp today as if something was amiss; even Elisa seemed toned down. The calm in the house was palpable which made Mui nervous. Elisa sat in the rocking chair next to the open window in the drawing room crocheting away a scarf, with a calm demeanour that Mui had not seen in ages. She peeked through the door of the other room. Elisa's eyes followed the slight disturbance, catching the eyes of her observer.

"Come here Mui," Elisa spoke in a low soft voice.

Her command forced Mui to come out of hiding and stand quietly in front of her, her hands firmly tucked behind her.

"We are leaving India and going back to Britain. I have called your aunt so that she can take you home; pack your belongings. You will leave in a few days." Elisa didn't justify her words further which left Mui in a state of panic.

"But what," Mui could barely speak but she sensed Elisa was not in a mood to talk so she just nodded.

"What is it child?" Elisa paused, giving Mui time to gather her words correctly, which was more than she could have got from her strict madam.

"When will you leave? Will you come back again? Do Emma and Edward know?" Mui spoke in a hurry.

"Slowly child, slowly," a smile broke on Elisa's face as she tried to calm the little girl.

"You have time to say your goodbyes Mui. I might not be available henceforth but I do want you to have a good life ahead."

Such kind words took Mui by surprise as Elisa shifted her attention from the little nanny to her crochet work, which by now had several imperfections.

"Yes, meemsaab," Mui left feeling a bit queasy.

Saying goodbye to Edward would be extremely difficult for her. The whole day she slogged throughout the house, doing her chores half-heartedly, fiddling with the idea of getting her scattered life back on track. Emma noticed the faraway look on Mui's face and was not shy to point it out loud.

"So, it seems you have heard of us leaving. You know, mother and I are so excited to finally go back home." Emma's words were not meant to please anyone other than herself, as Mui's face dropped even further.

"Mui, are we leaving?" Edward pulled her hand with a clueless expression.

"Yes, we are Edward, and you better get used to not having Mui around," Emma spoke even before Mui could comfort him. Tears welled up in Edward's eyes as he gave a loud cry and held Mui from her waist just sobbing away; Mui held him softly and went on her knees to be at his level and looked at his adorable face.

"There, there Edward. It's going to be alright. We are friends and will always be. So whenever you feel you need me, you look at the sky and you will find me among the clouds" Mui's words were so comforting that Edward stopped crying at once.

"You will be in the clouds?"

"Yes, I will be, and even in the rainbows," Mui said smiling.

"I will miss you too Emma," Mui said looking at her directly.

Emma's expression changed as she took offence to such a statement by a nanny.

"Your gardener friend is leaving too, and he could even be gone by the time we finish this conversation," she remarked stone- heartedly and left without giving a second thought to the hurt and pain she might have caused.

Mui tried to catch her breath as the sudden news took her by surprise; Edward looked at her terrified.

"I'm sorry Edward, I have to go." Even Edward knew this was important, so he let her go without stopping her. She ran towards the door and rushed out from the house towards her room as she knew Luca would be waiting there only. Barely looking up she bumped into him. He caught her, softly holding her shaken up body with his hands.

Words couldn't reach their lips as tears welled up in their eyes. By the look in his eyes she knew it was time for him to go.

"Luca..." Mui dropped to the ground crying as Luca held her hands and sat next to her frail body.

"I will always be there with you, miaamico." He just looked her in the eyes with the strength that she needed and pulled her up. They both walked silently to her room, tightly holding each other's hand as if to never let go. She looked into his eyes trying to give him strength to part with cherished memories.

Luca gave Mui one last look and scrounged for something in his pocket till he found what he was looking for.He smiled at his little friend and thrust hundred rupees, all in change, into her hand; Angus had managed to collect this from the entire camp. Coins fell on the ground making clinking noises, as the money was too much for her tiny hands to hold. She glanced at the money and then at her friend.Her heart sank as she dropped the money on the floor and hugged Luca.

"Look after yourself Mui; I will always remember you my dear friend,"his words had a touch of finality and such affection that Mui couldn't bear the excruciating pain that gripped her heart. He gathered the scattered money and gave it to Mui to keep safe.

"Don't forget your freedom Luca; we will all have it one day." Luca could only nod at the wise words spoken with such warmth.He left with a sinking heart, not even having the strength to look back as he kept walking, till he was far from her sight.

"I will be ok Luca," she muttered to herself as the prisoner left her sight and vanished from her life never to return again.

INCINERATOR & STORE: PHASI GHAR

The incinerator and store were built in 1943 on the outskirts of the PoW camp for burning waste material. The area was also known as Phasi Ghar (gallows) by the locals probably due to the unique shape of the structure which looked like a hang-man's pole.

www.ingramcontent.com/pod-product-compliance
Lightning Source LLC
LaVergne TN
LVHW091605170726
843492LV00007B/2259